Katz advanced cautiously

The Phoenix Force commander scanned the beer hall and then moved toward the trio of assailants. Two were obviously dead. The third man was curled in a fetal position, both hands clasped to his bullet-riddled lower abdomen.

The Israeli knelt by the terrorist. The man did not appear to be breathing. Katz returned his P-226 pistol to shoulder leather before checking for a pulse.

Suddenly the wounded terrorist rolled on his back. He gripped a compact Hi-Standard derringer in his bloody hands. A twisted smile slithered across his pain-racked face as he pointed the tiny two-shot pistol at Katzenelenbogen.

The bullet slammed into his left temple.

Mack Bolan's

PHOENIX FORCE

PHOENIX FORCE

The Doomsday Syndrome

Gar Wilson

A GOLD EAGLE BOOK FROM
WORLDWIDE

TORONTO · NEW YORK · LONDON · PARIS
AMSTERDAM · STOCKHOLM · HAMBURG
ATHENS · MILAN · TOKYO · SYDNEY

First edition July 1986

ISBN 0-373-61324-5

Special thanks and acknowledgment to William Fieldhouse
for his contribution to this work.

Printed in Canada

1

Boris Igorovich Churanov, Michel Zeleny and Bohumil Ryze sat at a table in the Kamen Kocka tavern on Siroka Street in Old Town, Prague. The three men were old friends; they had first met in 1968, shortly after the Soviet invasion of Czechoslovakia.

But they had not been part of that violent takeover. They were engineers—builders not destroyers—who were instrumental in the reconstruction program that resulted from the Soviet wave of destruction. Regularly after work they had shared a mutual appreciation for *cerveny*—beer—Tchaikovsky and Slavic women around their usual table in the tavern.

As an officer in the Soviet army's 423rd Corps of Engineers, Boris Churanov had no emotional ties to Czechoslovakia. But although he was technically a Communist, he also had no love or respect for either the Politburo or the Kremlin.

Zeleny and Ryze shared their Soviet comrade's political caprice but, then, they were Czechs. They had witnessed the Russian invasion of their homeland and they knew how severely the Czechoslovakian attempt to establish self-rule had been crushed.

The Czechs had thought they held all the cards. They had tried to establish a democratic socialist government independent of the USSR at a time when Russia was speaking out against American involvement in Southeast Asia. They had been sure that the Soviets could not publicly oppose such a move.

The Czechs had gambled and lost. The Kremlin did not give a damn about world opinion. The word "hypocrisy" did not translate into Russian. The people of Czechoslovakia learned a grim lesson when the Russian tanks rumbled into Prague: the Soviet Union owned their country and it would not tolerate any form of dissension.

Now, almost twenty years later, the trio were reunited. Churanov had been chosen to assist in the restoration of the Tyn Church and the Betlemska Chapel, both of which were located in the Old Town Square of Prague. Moscow realized that an iron fist was not enough to hold the reins of power. By helping to restore two famous churches of historical importance, the Czechs would see that the Kremlin cared about its East European comrades.

Churanov was an ideal choice for this assignment. He was familiar with Prague and spoke Czech fluently. If the Kremlin knew that Churanov was not the dedicated supporter of Soviet Communism that he appeared to be, then it apparently did not care.

The trio sat at their same table in the Kamen Kocka tavern. Very little had changed since the men had first visited the bar. The beer was still thirst quenching and the same greasy oilcloths covered the tables, and the owner, Milan Branislav, who was descended from a long line of innkeepers, beer brewers and bootleggers, continued to violate the state's regulations of collectivism.

Branislav covertly brewed his own beer and failed to report its sale to the authorities. He also served favored customers after the state's legal closing time. The windows of the tavern were thick and darkly tinted, with good reason. They prevented unwanted patrols from becoming too curious. Branislav also used kerosene lamps after midnight to keep the tavern's electricity consumption on par with similar establishments.

Branislav knew such actions seemed petty by Western standards, yet such behavior was quite daring in a Communist state functioning under the yoke of the Soviet Union. Complete control of goods and services has always been an essential part of Marxism, and personal profit is regarded as an act of piracy against the state. Branislav's minor bootlegging and extra business after hours made him eligible for several years in a labor camp if he was caught.

Naturally he only allowed trusted friends to participate in this clandestine business. Besides Churanov, Zeleny and Ryze, there were only five other customers in the tavern that night. Two farmers sat across the room, discussing crops, the collective-farm system and women. The Hladky brothers sat at another table with their guest, the only stranger in the Kamen Kocka Tavern.

Felix and Ludwig Hladky operated a small hotel on the outskirts of Prague. The Hladky brothers were strongly opposed to Communism. They carefully screened the guests at their hotel, preferring to rent to other anti-Communists. For obvious reasons they did not want their visitors to include STB agents from the Czech Intelligence Service, or members of the dreaded KGB.

They had invited Heinrich Kohler to the tavern despite the fact that they suspected Kohler was using a false name. They had considered the possibility that Kohler was an agent for the BND, the main intelligence network of West Germany, or that he worked for the American CIA or the British SIS. But the Hladky brothers were certain of one thing: the man's Bavarian accent was genuine, so they felt confident that Kohler was not a Communist East German operative.

"You seem apprehensive, Herr Kohler," Ludwig Hladky remarked as he tried once again to draw the German into conversation.

"I'm just tired," Kohler assured him, sliding his chair back from the table. "I really must return to the hotel and get some rest."

"We're leaving in a few minutes..." Felix Hladky began.

"Don't hurry for my sake," the German urged as he stood. "I can find my way back to the hotel. All my papers are in order. If the police stop me, I'm sure I can convince them that I'm a harmless tourist. Please enjoy yourselves, and thank you for a pleasant evening. *Dobrou noc.*"

"*Dobrou noc,* Herr Kohler," the Hladky brothers said in unison.

Felix Hladky frowned as he watched Kohler move toward the door.

"What is wrong, Felix?" Ludwig inquired.

"I wonder if Kohler can be trusted?" Felix answered. "We know nothing about the man, but he knows enough about us to have us both arrested. In fact, everyone in this room could be in danger. Especially Milan."

"You worry without need, my brother," Ludwig assured him. "Kohler is a German national. *Ano?*"

"*Mozna,*" Felix said with a shrug. "Perhaps, but he could be an East German agent, or even a member of the KGB. It has been said that hundreds of Communist agents have infiltrated the Federal Republic of Germany. These spies have been trained to pass as native citizens. They learn the customs and politics of the country and how to speak the language with the proper accent. How do we know that Kohler isn't such a spy?"

"Don't be paranoid," Ludwig scolded, although privately he shared his brother's fears.

"We have a reason to be paranoid," Felix insisted.

"Is something wrong, my friends?" Milan Branislav asked as he approached their table. The chubby innkeeper was usually cheerful and pleasant, but he was obviously concerned by the expressions on the brothers' faces.

"Ne, Milan," Ludwig assured him. "My brother and I simply disagree about something."

"I heard you mention the KGB," Branislav began. "Certainly you are not worried about Boris Churanov. He's an old friend and I trust him as much as any Czech."

"We know that, Milan," Ludwig said. "You are always very careful about who you allow in the Kamen Kocka."

"I do my best," Branislav stated. "Although I'm not familiar with your German friend. You should tell me when you invite someone to join us after regular business hours."

"We didn't know how long he would stay," Felix explained.

"He is careless, whoever he is," Branislav remarked as he reached down beside the table and lifted a small, cloth overnight bag. "He must have left this."

"I believe that does belong to Kohler," Felix stated. "He's staying at the hotel. We'll take it to him and—"

Before Felix Hladky could finish his sentence the overnight bag exploded. Bloody pieces of Milan Branislav were splattered in every direction. Felix and Ludwig were decapitated, their heads brutally ripped from their necks.

The force of the explosion rocked the whole tavern. Furniture was smashed into flying splinters. Shattered glass became bullets with razor tips, piercing flesh, entering gaping mouths and stabbing eyeballs. Yet none of the customers screamed. They were already dead, pulverized by the abrupt fury of the explosion.

On the other side of the street Heinrich Kohler lowered a small pair of binoculars. Flames danced inside what remained of the tavern. Every window had been blown out by the blast. The German smiled thinly and nodded with approval. He put the binoculars in a coat pocket and began to walk toward his hotel.

2

Rafael Encizo sat up in the bed with his back propped against two pillows. Although his head was thickly bandaged, a wide smile split the Cuban's swarthy face. The four members of Phoenix Force standing at the foot of the bed were greatly relieved to see that Encizo's condition had improved dramatically since their last visit.

"Should have known a bullet couldn't do any real damage to a thick skull like yours," David McCarter said with mock gruffness.

McCarter had been as concerned about Encizo as the others had been, but open sentimental gestures were not part of his nature. His Phoenix Force comrade had been wounded during a recent mission in France. The near-fatal bullet had struck the Cuban's cranium and put him in a coma. For days he had teetered between life and death.

Phoenix Force had rushed Encizo to the USAEUR— United States Army in Europe—Hospital in Nuremberg, Germany. A doctor there had determined that Encizo's skull had been fractured and that he had a concussion. However, there was no evidence of brain damage and the surgery had gone well.

Rafael Encizo was not an easy man to kill. As a teenager he had fought the Communists in Havana and in 1961 had participated in the disastrous Bay of Pigs Invasion. He was captured and sent to El Príncipe, Castro's notorious political prison. Encizo survived starvation, abuse and torture without breaking. He never gave up, and when a guard was finally careless with Encizo the Cuban broke the man's neck and escaped to the United States.

The Cuban crusader became a naturalized U.S. citizen and worked in various unusual professions. He was a diving instructor in Florida. He searched for sunken treasure off the coast of Puerto Rico. And he hired himself out as a professional bodyguard across most of the United States. He was an insurance investigator specializing in maritime claims when he was asked to join Phoenix Force. Encizo's unique background, and the skill he had developed as a frogman, knife fighter, small-arms expert and master at break and entry, made him an ideal choice for this unusual elite fighting unit.

There had never been a team quite like Phoenix Force. Mack Bolan, alias the Executioner, had personally chosen the five men for this special operations commando unit. They were selected from the most highly trained and the most experienced fighting men of the free world.

Bolan had been the key figure at Stony Man, an organization created by secret executive order. As part of this group, Phoenix Force was formed to take direct action against international terrorism. The Executioner's group specialized in seek-and-destroy operations; they were good at their job.

Phoenix Force had tangled with an amazing assortment of terrorist groups, enemy agents and international criminal organizations. Their missions had been one hundred percent successful. However, both Phoenix Force and Stony Man had paid dearly for this success.

An enemy raid on Stony Man headquarters took the life of Andrzej Konzaki, the resident weapons expert. Aaron Kurtzman, the computer wizard, was seriously wounded by a bullet to the spine. He was confined to a wheelchair, crippled for life.

Phoenix Force had also suffered a casualty among the team's own members. Keio Ohara, one of the original five men chosen by the Executioner, was killed during a mission against the sinister Black Alchemist terrorists. Yet Stony Man and Phoenix Force had survived these terrible ordeals. Death had nearly claimed Rafael Encizo, but the tough Cuban had once again escaped the clutches of the Grim Reaper and now appeared to be on the road to recovery.

"Sorry we weren't here when you awoke from the coma," Yakov Katzenelenbogen told Encizo.

Katz did not fit the image of a supercommando. Middle-aged and slightly paunchy, he looked more like a college professor or a businessman approaching retirement. His gentle blue eyes and ready smile suggested that he was a kind, understanding man. His soft-spoken voice was articulate and cultured. Only the fact that this scholarly gentleman's right arm had been amputated at the elbow suggested that he led a somewhat more adventurous life.

The accident had occurred during the Six Day War. Katz had lost the arm in an explosion that also claimed the life of his only son. It had been one of the bloodiest battles that Yakov Katzenelenbogen had encountered. His incredible career as a soldier, espionage agent and antiterrorist had started during his teens in Europe. His family were Russian Jews living in France. They were double damned by the Nazi occupation. Most of the Katzenelenbogen family died in Hitler's death camps, but Katz had joined the resistance movement. An accomplished linguist who spoke French, German, English and Russian fluently, he was the ideal candidate to infiltrate enemy lines posing as a native. It was not long before the American OSS recruited the talented youth for their own covert operations.

After World War II, Katz moved to Palestine and joined Israel's struggle for independence. He soon became an officer in the Israeli army. After the Six Day War he was promoted to full colonel. In spite of his handicap, Katz did not retire from field operations. He became more involved in espionage missions for the Mossad, Israel's main intelligence organization.

In an effort to increase cooperation with Western nations, Israel agreed to loan Katz to the CIA, British SIS, West German BND and the French Sûreté. When Mack Bolan learned of Katz's extraordinary experience and skills, he knew that he had found the unit commander for Phoenix Force.

"Hal told me you guys had to rush off on urgent business," Encizo assured Katz.

"Brognola was here?" McCarter inquired with surprise.

Hal Brognola had always been the go-between for Stony Man and the White House. After the Executioner was forced to leave the organization, Brognola became chief of operations and head of Stony Man.

"Yeah," Encizo said with a grin. "Hal was here when I woke up after surgery. He told the doctor he wanted to know all the details of my condition. And he said I should get everything I need or want."

"Bloody miracle we found you in bed by yourself," McCarter snorted.

The fox-faced Briton could rarely resist an opportunity to voice a sarcastic remark. McCarter's sharp tongue and wry sense of humor was as much a part of his personality as his exceptional courage, phenomenal skill and fierce dedication to duty.

David McCarter was a living war machine. A veteran of the fabulous Special Air Service, McCarter had seen action in the streets of Belfast and the mountains of Oman. He had been a special observer in Vietnam and had participated in a covert police action in Hong Kong. Sergeant McCarter had also been one of the SAS commandos and had participated in Operation Nimrod, the spectacular 1980 raid on the Iranian Embassy in London.

A superb pilot, pistol champion and an expert in virtually every form of combat, McCarter was a highly trained and uniquely gifted warrior. He was addicted to adventure. The battlefield was his natural element and combating terrorism was what he did best in life.

"I'm just sorry I've missed out on a couple of missions." Encizo sighed as he propped himself up on an elbow. "Hal told me you guys had to make an emergency trip to South Africa and then back to the States."

"Yeah, I was really thrilled about the South African one," Calvin James said dryly.

James was a tall, black man with the well-toned physique of an athlete. He had been born and raised in the formidable south side of Chicago, which explained why James was already a skilled street fighter and knife artist before he enlisted in the Navy at the age of seventeen. Survival training begins at childhood on the south side.

Trained as a hospital corpsman, James joined an elite Sea, Air and Land team. As a SEAL, the black commando became proficient in small arms, parachuting, underwater combat and jungle survival. He put all of these skills to practical use in Vietnam. James left the Navy with an honorable discharge and numerous decorations for valor and distinguished service.

Calvin James pursued a career in medicine and enrolled at UCLA on the GI bill. Then fate threw a cruel curve into James's plans. His mother and sister were both victims of brutal slayings. This convinced James to seek a new career in law enforcement.

James joined the San Francisco Police Department and soon became a member of the Special Weapons and Tactics team. He was actually involved in a SWAT assignment when Phoenix Force recruited him for a special mission that required his knowledge of chemistry. James had remained with Phoenix Force ever since.

"Was it really that bad for you in South Africa?" Encizo inquired.

"Not really," James admitted. "There weren't too many Simon Legree types, but their policy of apartheid sure didn't make me happy."

"Hal told me the mission went smooth as glass," the Cuban remarked.

"Brognola wasn't with us in Africa," Gary Manning replied. "There were a few bumps on the road before we completed the mission."

The bumps Manning referred to had included two deadly ambushes by murderous terrorists and two dangerous raids against separate enemy strongholds. Manning was not the sort to get overexcited or to exaggerate. He was a calm man by nature, with an organized mind and incredible willpower.

The Canadian member of Phoenix Force was built like the stereotypical lumberjack, the result of hours of weight lifting, rugby and long-distance running. Manning's physical and mental endurance were extraordinary. His determination and his meticulousness had made him a successful businessman in Canada. It had also made him one of the best demolitions experts in the world.

A former lieutenant in the Canadian army, Manning had been an observer in Vietnam. He was attached to the covert Special Observation Group and worked with the American 5th Special Forces.

Manning participated in several missions behind enemy lines. He was an excellent rifle marksman and became an adept sniper as well as an explosives wizard. Manning was awarded the Silver Star, one of the few Canadian citizens to receive this honor during the Vietnam conflict.

After Nam, Manning was recruited by the intelligence branch of the Royal Canadian Mounted Police. Concerned about the growing threat of international terrorism, the RCMP had planned to create an antiterrorist section. Manning was sent to West Germany to train with the newly formed GSG-9 squad. The Canadian dynamo gained new skills and firsthand experience in urban guerrilla warfare.

The RCMP was forced out of the espionage business following several scandals involving the abuse of power. The Canadian SIS offered Manning a desk job as an adviser. Manning decided that if he was going to be stuck in an office, he might as well make a decent profit in the process. He entered the business world and soon became a junior executive with North American International. However, when Manning was asked to join Phoenix Force he eagerly accepted the opportunity to once again battle the enemies of freedom and civilization.

"I half expected to see Hahn with you guys," Encizo commented. "Brognola told me that Karl has filled in for me."

"Hahn had to be debriefed by the BND," Katz explained. "Karl is still one of their agents. But that's no problem. We can trust him to keep our security intact."

"Karl's a good man," Encizo confirmed. "You were lucky to get somebody we've worked with in the past."

"Yeah," James said with a shrug. "But we'll be glad when you're back on your feet and fit for duty, my man."

"That'll make two of us," the Cuban assured him.

"How long will you be loafing around in this rest home," McCarter inquired.

"Doc Towers told me that I need at least two months to be sure my head heals properly." Encizo frowned. "He said something about possible side effects after the surgery."

"Better listen to him, Rafael," Katz urged. "He is one of the best surgeons in the United States Army. He knows what he's talking about."

"Maybe," Encizo said with a shrug, "but he's been hinting that I ought to retire. However, he hasn't asked too many questions about my profession. Probably figures I wouldn't tell him the truth, anyway."

"I'm sure he thinks we're CIA," Manning remarked. "And it's probably okay if he continues to think that."

"It would be okay with me if he let me get the hell out of here," the Cuban muttered.

"You can't expect to heal overnight," James, the unit medic, told him. "Maybe you don't realize it, but you damn near got killed in France. If that bullet had hit a half inch to the left, we wouldn't be able to talk to you without a Ouija board, man."

"And you've got more to consider than your own life, Rafael," Katz added. "Every member of Phoenix Force must be in top physical condition. We must be able to rely on one another and not have to worry about whether one of us is fit enough for a mission. I'm sure I don't have to remind you that every time we embark on an assignment, hundreds of innocent lives are at stake. That's too great a responsibility to risk just because you're eager to get back into action."

"I know," Encizo was forced to admit. "I guess all I can do is hope that Phoenix Force doesn't get another mission before I'm well enough to participate."

"I know how you feel, mate," McCarter said with sincere sympathy. "Remember that time in Greece when I caught a bullet in the arm? I wasn't able to take part in the final raid on Krio Island because of that damn flesh wound."

"Yeah," Encizo recalled. "But you didn't have to lie around in a hospital and miss two entire missions."

"So you're not as lucky as I am," the Briton said with a shrug. "Not much I can do about that."

Knuckles rapped on the door and then Captain Collins, an Army intelligence officer, entered the room. Collins had been assigned to act as go-between for Phoenix Force and Hal Brognola. Of course, Collins did not know any details or the real names of anyone involved with Stony Man. He simply received information and passed it on to the five mysterious strangers.

"Mr. Warburg?" Collins began, referring to Katz by his current cover name. "A special message has come in for you on a private line."

"I'll be right there," Katz replied with a nod.

"Oh, shit," Encizo groaned. "Not again."

3

Yakov Katzenelenbogen followed Captain Collins through the hospital corridor to a private office. The captain took a key ring from his pocket and moved toward a steel cabinet. After unlocking two locks, he was finally able to open the bottom drawer.

"Whatever the message is," Katz began, "my partners should be here, too. I don't keep any secrets from them."

"I certainly wouldn't accuse you of being a liar, sir," Collins began as he removed a black object that resembled a case for a portable typewriter. "And I must admit I don't know exactly what your group is involved with, but I would imagine anybody who has been involved in intelligence operations as long as you've probably been in this business keeps secrets without even realizing it."

"You might be right, Captain," the Israeli colonel confessed. He was pleased with Collins. The young officer seemed to understand the nature of intelligence.

"Well," Collins replied. "I have orders to relay all information directly to you, Mr. Warburg. What you choose to do with it is totally up to you."

"What have you got for me?" the Phoenix Force commander asked.

"I'm not sure," the captain answered as he opened the case to reveal a compact computer complete with a flat keyboard and a narrow viewscreen. "I received a message on a secure telephone line. I was instructed to plug the call into this XL-Nine Hundred unit. I knew that meant the message was for you. Whatever the information is, it was transmitted into the computer at high speed in a numerical code. I'm afraid that I can't decipher it, but the word 'buttercup' appeared on the screen at the end of the transmission. I assume you know what that means, Mr. Warburg?''

"Oh, yes," Katz assured him. "Is this code printed on a diskette, Captain?''

"Yes, sir," Collins confirmed. "I'll take it out of the machine. The XL-Nine Hundred isn't designed for translating codes, but I might be able to help you if you need to get the message translated.''

"No, thanks," Katz replied. "We'll manage.''

Captain Collins removed the diskette and handed it to the Phoenix Force commander.

"Good luck, sir," he said.

"Thank you, Captain," Katz replied. "We can always use it.''

The men of Phoenix Force, sans Rafael Encizo, left the hospital to meet with "buttercup." This was the unlikely code name that Hal Brognola had previously given to Karl Hahn. The four members of Phoenix Force met with Hahn at the Telemann Antique Shop in the small city of Schwabach, about ten kilometers south of Nuremberg. The shop owner, Otto Telemann, was a retired police officer who earned five hundred marks a month, tax-free, for allowing his establishment to be used as a part-time safe house for the BND.

Karl Hahn greeted the men of Phoenix Force with enthusiasm. The well-muscled German intel officer did not look like a buttercup, or any other type of flower for that matter. Hahn was a rugged individual with close-cropped brown hair, green eyes and a keen mind.

Hahn had formerly been a member of GSG-9, the elite antiterrorist unit created in 1972 by the West German government after the so-called Munich Massacre. The eyes of the world had been focused on Germany that year when Israeli athletes were slaughtered by Black September terrorists at the Olympic Village. The efficiency of the GSG-9 was revealed to the world in 1977 when a sixty-man commando team rescued eighty-six hostages from a hijacked Lufthansa Boeing 747 being held in Mogadishu, Somalia. The raid was a stunning success, and it established that the GSG-9 was one of the finest commando units in the world.

Karl Hahn had participated in the Mogadishu raid, but he had earned most of his field experience in missions within the Federal Republic of Germany itself. During the early to mid-seventies, numerous terrorist groups were active in West Germany. The Baader-Meinhof gang, the Second June Movement, the German Red Army Faction and several Palestinian groups were spreading havoc across the country at an alarming rate. Hahn was among the GSG-9 forces that combated the minions of destruction.

The Red Army Faction made the mistake of capturing and torturing Klaus Hausberg, a fellow GSG-9 operative and Hahn's best friend. Karl Hahn retaliated by hunting down the terrorists in a vendetta that lasted more than a year before his superiors learned that Hahn had executed at least eight terrorists.

The German was dismissed from the antiterrorist organization, but he was too talented for his skills to go untapped. The BND recruited Hahn and trained him for covert assignments behind the iron curtain in East Germany and Czechoslovakia. He was stationed in Turkey as a case officer when he first met and worked with Phoenix Force.

Karl Hahn's special skills made him a very valuable operative. He had been a foreign-exchange student in the United States and had studied computer electronics at UCLA. Hahn spoke three languages fluently and had a good working vocabulary of Czechoslovakian and Russian. He had also developed a deadly knack for improvising when he needed a weapon in an emergency. A rolled-up newspaper or a ballpoint pen could be lethal in the hands of Karl Hahn.

"I didn't expect to hear from you so soon," Hahn confessed as he escorted the four Phoenix Force fighters through the antique shop. "How's Rafael?"

"He's out of the coma and appears to be healing nicely," Katz replied. "But he isn't ready to join us on assignment yet."

"Does that mean we'll be working together again?" Hahn asked, raising his eyebrows. "You guys nearly got me killed the last time. I guess this will give you a chance to finish the job."

"You don't have to come along if you don't want to," Gary Manning assured him.

"Don't be crazy," Hahn said gruffly. "The BND hasn't given me a new assignment yet, so I'm sure I can get their authorization for another mission."

"We're not sure we've got a mission, Karl," Katz announced as he took the diskette from his pocket. "Perhaps you can find out for us."

"Coded message, eh?" Hahn remarked, taking the diskette. "It's a XL-Nine Hundred unit, so it's a numerical code. Shouldn't be too difficult to break if I can figure out the key word or number combination."

"Your code name 'buttercup' was at the end of the message," Manning told him. "Does that help?"

"Well, I know that I'd be wasting my time by trying 'buttercup' as a key phrase," the German agent said with a shrug.

He moved to a back room that contained a remarkable assortment of hi-tech equipment. Two computers were mounted on desks. One was linked to a word processor and a 3M copying machine. An infinity transmitter and an ultrahigh-frequency radio receiver were positioned at one corner of the room. The four men of Phoenix Force were not even sure what some of the machines would be used for. They stood clear of the gadgets, afraid that their very presence might cause something to malfunction.

Hahn was perfectly at home with the computers. He fed the diskette into one of the machines and punched two buttons on the keyboard. Yellow letters appeared on the green viewscreen—a request for additional data.

"Now we need the key phrase," Hahn mused, speaking to himself more than to the four commandos. "Probably a word. Numerical combinations are easier to decipher with a computer because you can run through a thousand variations in less than a minute. Words are much more time-consuming, especially when you consider the fact that the key could be in any language."

His fingers danced across the keyboard. H-A-H-N appeared on the screen. The word "INCORRECT" flashed in response to his first attempt. Hahn was not surprised. It was highly unlikely that his name would be used for the key. His first name, Karl, was also far too common in Germany. He quickly dismissed that possibility and tried a different route. Perhaps the key was the location where he had first assisted Phoenix Force. Hahn punched in I-S-T-A-N-B-U-L. Once again the screen flashed "INCORRECT."

Hahn was about to try something different, but decided to play on a hunch. Perhaps the key word was the ancient name for Istanbul, the name used when it was the capital of the Holy Roman Empire. He punched in C-O-N-S-T-A-N-T-I-N-O-P-L-E. A row of numbers immediately appeared on the screen. Hahn smiled and punched in the numbers. The computer translating device did the rest. A brief message in English appeared on the screen.

"'Send two men to the Wagner Beer Hall, Munich,'" Hahn said, reading the message aloud. "'Nine hundred hours on the twenty-third.'"

"That's all?" McCarter asked.

"That's it," Hahn confirmed. "Unless there's something cryptic in the sentence itself—wait, there's something else."

A second message appeared on the screen.

"'Wear brown hats,'" Hahn announced. "Is that significant?"

"I guess that's how our contact will recognize us," Katz said with a shrug. "Of course, we never use the exact time or dates for messages of this nature. Nine hundred hours actually means twenty-one hundred hours. That's 9:00 P.M. and not A.M."

"Yeah," Gary Manning agreed. "And the twenty-third is tomorrow. That means we're supposed to meet somebody at the Wagner Beer Hall tonight."

"*Two* of us are supposed to meet somebody at the beer hall," Katz commented. "Karl, you're familiar with Munich, aren't you?"

"Naturally," the German agent replied with a smile. "Munich is the cultural capital of Bavaria. It's the best place in the world to celebrate the Oktoberfest."

"Well, this ain't October," James remarked. "And we're not going to a festival."

"The Oktoberfest isn't held in October," Hahn explained. "It's celebrated in the last two weeks of September."

"I remember," Gary Manning commented. "The Oktoberfest is a country fair, a Mardi Gras and a Viking orgy all rolled into one."

"Sounds bloody wonderful," McCarter said with a grin.

"You'd probably be bored by it," Hahn told him. "It's unlikely that anyone would shoot at you."

"Oh," McCarter said, shrugging.

"Karl and I will meet with the contact and try to find out what's going on," Katz declared. "The rest of you can get our gear so we can move out as soon as possible in case we've got a hot assignment."

"What about backup at the meet?" James asked.

"Our orders call for two men to go to the beer hall tonight," Katz replied. "That means *just two* men."

"Watch yourself," McCarter advised. "There's something odd about this business. Seems to be more cloak-and-dagger than the jobs we usually get."

"That's why Karl and I will make contact," Katz replied. "We've got more experience at this sort of thing than the rest of you."

THE BAVARIAN BEER HALL has traditionally been a place of social gathering similar to the British pub or the Japanese teahouse. But it is perhaps the American pool hall that most closely resembles a *Hofbrauhaus*. The good-natured camaraderie and fellowship of the beer hall is very informal.

Yakov Katzenelenbogen and Karl Hahn sat on one of the wide benches at a long table inside the Wagner Beer Hall. Virtually all of the customers were men. A group of Germans at the next table cheerfully sang a Bavarian drinking ballad. Others soon joined in song. The waiters, Italian immigrants, hurried from table to table, carrying tall liter mugs. They scooped up empty steins and replaced them with full mugs of fresh brew.

One of the waiters noticed that Katz was not drinking his beer and that Hahn had only sipped at his. Otherwise the pair had not attracted any attention. Hahn had purchased a dark-tan cloth cap and Katz wore a brown hat with a battered rim. The weather was cloudy that night, so no one thought it odd that both men wore hats. Besides, the autumn night was chilly.

Katz's loose-fitting coat concealed a SIG-Sauer P-226 double-action automatic in a shoulder holster under his right arm. He also carried a .380 Beretta in a pancake holster at the small of his spine for backup. Hahn wore a raincoat that easily hid his Walther P-5 in its shoulder leather. A tiny .25 caliber Bauer automatic was also hidden in one of the coat's pockets.

"Maybe we've been stood up," Hahn remarked, speaking English in case anyone was listening.

"Maybe," Katz replied as he pulled back his right sleeve to reveal a lifelike prosthesis attached to the stump of his arm. Katz wore a pair of pearl-gray gloves to cover the steel and plastic fingers. Unless one noticed that the fingers of his right hand were unusually stiff, it was almost impossible to suspect that Katz was an amputee. He glanced at the luminous face of the watch strapped to the wrist of his prosthesis.

"It's 9:30," the Israeli announced. "We'll wait five minutes. If someone doesn't show by then, we'll head back to your safe house and wait for new orders."

"Perhaps we misunderstood the instructions," Hahn suggested.

"Maybe not," Katz remarked as two men approached their table.

The strangers looked as though they had just stepped out of the *Late Show*. One man was tall with black hair and a trim mustache. His partner was almost a head shorter and at least five years older. Both men wore tan coats and brown fedoras.

"Good evening, gentlemen," the tall man greeted them, speaking English with a heavy guttural accent. Katz, the expert linguist, was unable to determine the man's native tongue, but he was certain it was not German.

"May we join you for a drink?" the other stranger asked.

"You're late," Katz replied.

"Late?" The shorter stranger raised his thick eyebrows. "Not really. We waited to be certain that you were the right men. Actually, we were early. Yes?"

The pair sat across the table from Katz and Hahn. The BND agent leaned forward and smiled at them as he spoke.

"You fellows keep your hands on the table," Hahn told them softly but threateningly. "I have a pistol in my hand and it is aimed at your bellies. Don't think that because this is a public place I won't shoot you both."

"What is the meaning of this?" the elder man demanded.

"Shooting someone under a table is not always very accurate, my friend," the tall man said calmly, although he kept his hands in clear view. "I doubt if you can be sure of a heart shot."

"But I'm sure to put a bullet in your guts or crotch," Hahn answered. "If that appeals to you, make your move, friend."

"I demand an explanation," the shorter man insisted.

"I suspect that my friend is concerned about your accent," Katz said with a shrug. "Slavic, isn't it?"

"They're Czechs," Hahn announced. "Central Bohemian dialect."

"Mluvite cesky?" the short man inquired, asking Hahn if he spoke Czechoslovakian.

"Ano," the German agent confirmed. *"Co si prejete?"*

"What we want is to discuss this matter without the threat of getting shot," the short Czech replied. "We're here for cooperation, not confrontation. The governments of both the United States and West Germany assured us that we could speak with you in safety."

"Then you've been told more than we have," Katz said. "I'm afraid we've had some problems with communications. I'll have to have a talk with my superiors about this."

"For now, let's talk," the shorter man urged. "I am Matus Meret and this is Josef Kohout. We're with the Czechoslovakian Embassy in Bonn."

"The last thing that either of your governments wants is to have two members of the Czech diplomatic corps murdered in a public beer hall in Munich," Kohout, the tall man, remarked.

"I'd rather it was the two of you than us," Hahn replied.

"I see," Meret mused. "You think perhaps we interfered with your communications and fed you misleading information in order to lay a trap for you."

"It crossed my mind," Katz admitted. "And I assume you fellows are members of the Czech Intelligence Service, right?"

"Yes," Meret confessed. "But you have no reason to be apprehensive. We must trust one another, gentlemen."

"In our line of work, trust is a very rare commodity," Katz stated. "Especially when dealing with agents from a Communist nation."

"We have far more reason to be suspicious of you," Kohout declared angrily.

"Why is that?" the Israeli asked.

"Over the past five months there have been numerous acts of terrorism within Czechoslovakia," Meret explained. "The targets of these acts of violence have varied, yet all have included one or more Russians among the victims."

"KGB?" Hahn inquired.

"We're STB agents," Kohout answered. "The Soviets don't give us any more information than they feel we're entitled to. However, at least two of the Russians killed by the terrorists were probably KGB agents. It is very unlikely that all the Russian victims were Soviet spies. The last Russian killed was an engineer named Churanov, and the others have included an agricultural adviser, a gymnastics coach and a man who designs washing machines in Kiev. Do those sound like KGB to you?''

"Possibly," Katz answered. "But not likely."

"The worst part is that a large number of innocent Czech civilians have been killed by the terrorists," Meret added. "For every Russian victim at least three Czech bystanders have been slain, as well. We Czechs would like to see the Soviets return to Mother Russia. Frankly, if only Russians were being killed we wouldn't be as upset as we are."

"No civilized man approves of killing innocent people," Katz assured him. "However, I don't see how this concerns us."

"You don't?" Meret inquired. "That should be obvious. The Soviets are convinced that the American CIA and the West German BND are responsible for these acts of terrorism in our country. It is a logical assumption, considering that the BND is the largest intelligence network in Western Europe and that it has always cooperated with the CIA. Now if you're familiar with the KGB, you know that it will retaliate and that it won't care if innocent Germans and Americans are killed."

"I'm surprised that that would upset the STB," Hahn said with a shrug.

"We do not want to cause an international incident involving either the the U.S. or West Germany. But the Czechoslovakian Intelligence Service must follow orders," Kohout declared. "The KGB pulls our strings. If those damn perfumed uncles decide to send us on missions against your countrymen, we'll have no choice but to obey."

Kohout and his STB comrades used the term "perfumed uncle" in reference to their Soviet overseers. "Uncle" referred to the KGB case officer's supervisory position. "Perfumed" resulted from the a habit practiced by many Soviet Communists: they douse themselves with strong perfume to mask the fact they have not bathed recently. It is considered a status symbol among some Russians because it suggests they are too busy working for the party to take time to bathe.

"You fellows admit you're STB and now you admit your organization is actually controlled by the Soviets." Hahn smiled. "That's rather like admitting you're KGB agents, isn't it?"

"We Czechs are not Bulgarians," Meret snapped. "We do not want to see the Soviet presence in our country increase because the Kremlin decides to escalate the cold war between the East and the West. You and I are on opposite sides, gentlemen, but that doesn't mean we don't *all* have reason to fear the Soviet reaction to the violence that threatens my country."

"There is indeed truth in what you say, Mr. Meret," Katz agreed. "But the terrorism you've told us about is taking place within Czechoslovakia. Surely you can appreciate the fact that we would have considerable trouble trying to operate in your country."

"And what makes you sure that we would have more success in dealing with these terrorists than the STB and the KGB had?" Hahn added.

"We were assured that we would meet with representatives of the CIA, the BND and another group," Meret began. "A very special group that has succeeded in missions against terrorist organizations, criminal societies and even the KGB. It is said to be an elite commando unit consisting of five experts, men who have succeeded when entire armies and the world's best intelligence networks have failed."

"Obviously somebody's missing from this meeting," Katz commented. "But let's say these supercommandos you mentioned are real. If they've participated in action against

the KGB, they'd have to be insane to go into Czechoslovakia.''

"This whole business could be a clever trap by the KGB,"
Hahn added. "What evidence do you have to prove otherwise?"

"Both the CIA and the American National Security
Agency have been gathering intelligence on this matter for
at least two months and I'm sure the BND has been doing
the same even longer," Meret replied. "Check with your
own people."

"All right," Katz began. "Now let's—"

Katz stopped in midsentence because he saw three men
approaching the table. The trio wore dark clothing and
black wool hats, which they began to pull down over their
faces. The hats were actually ski masks. The three men
reached inside their coats for weapons.

"Down!" Katz shouted as he threw himself to the floor.

Hahn immediately followed the Israeli's example. The
muffled report of silenced weapons coughed violently.
Startled customers seated at nearby tables cried out. Feet
hammered the floorboards as frightened patrons bolted
from their seats and stampeded toward the nearest exits.

Josef Kohout fell forward and landed across the table. His
nose was smashed and bleeding heavily, but Kohout did not
care. Half a dozen 9 mm parabellum slugs had torn into his
back. The STB officer's spine was shattered and two bullets had drilled into his lungs and severed the aorta. Kohout's body jerked weakly as though it were a marionette
being manipulated by a feeble puppet master. Blood gushed
from Kohout's open mouth as he slumped, lifeless, to the
floor.

Matus Meret followed his comrade to the floor. Blood
splurted from the Czech's upper right arm.

Katz barely glanced at the wounded man. He had already drawn his P-226 autoloader from shoulder leather and

his attention was locked on the advancing gunmen. If the assailants were not dealt with quickly Katz and Hahn would not live long enough to help Meret.

Katz peered up from the table at the three gunners. They were armed with machine pistols equipped with sound suppressors. They continued to fire as they approached the table. Bullets splintered wood and sizzled above the Israeli's head as he braced his left arm and the fist holding the SIG-Sauer pistol across the bench.

The Phoenix pro opened fire, squeezing off three rounds from the double-action autoloader. One gunman caught two 115 9 mm slugs in the chest. He toppled backward, arms flung wide. The gunman fell into one of his comrades and both men dropped to the floor. The third triggerman was no happier than his partners. He was doubled up in agony with Katz's third bullet buried in his large intestine.

The uninjured gunman fell to one knee and roughly shoved his dying comrade aside. He hastily aimed his Ingram M-10 machine pistol at Katz's position. But the gunman failed to notice Karl Hahn. The BND agent held his Walther P-5 in a two-handed weaver grip and aimed around the corner of the table.

Hahn triggered his pistol, firing two rounds. Both 9 mm messengers crashed into the gunman's face. One parabellum pierced the guy's ski mask, split a cheekbone and shattered the left jawbone joint. The other bullet struck the bridge of his nose and burned through the sinus to his brain. The would-be assassin dropped dead with the Ingram locked in his fists in a death grip.

"I think that's all of them," Hahn announced as he started to rise.

A volley of full-auto gunfire erupted from the opposite end of the beer hall. Bullets pelted a stone pillar near Hahn's head. A stray round bit into the tabletop in front of the German agent. Hahn quickly dropped to the floor. His right elbow struck the edge of the bench. Pain shot through the ulna nerve in his arm. Hahn's fingers popped open and the Walter seemed to hop from his grasp like a metallic frog.

"Think again," Katz muttered sourly.

4

At least three new attackers had joined the party. They approached from the west end of the beer hall. It was difficult to tell how many assailants were among the second hit team. The enemy were crouched low and they scurried from table to table for cover. The poor light from the fifty-watt bulbs overhead hindered the Phoenix warriors' attempts to take a head count—not that any of the aggressors were foolish enough to actually raise their heads.

The Phoenix Force commander heard Matus Meret moan. The wounded Czech lay on his side, clutching his upper right arm as he tried to stop the bleeding with fingertip pressure to the brachial artery. Meret was not going to be of any help in the firefight. Even if he had not been wounded, the Czech intel officer probably would not have been of much assistance. The STB had a reputation for being well trained in intelligence gathering, in leaking false information and black propoganda to the Western press and in electronic eavesdropping. However, the Soviets had not encouraged the agents of their satellite countries to learn survival or combat techniques. The Communists had sciezed control of the Soviet Union during a revolution, and they were not about to let such an event threaten their own rule.

Meret would have to wait. The STB agent would not bleed to death as long as he did not catch any more bullets. Katz moved along the table, changing positions to confuse the enemy. The Israeli reached the end and quickly scrambled to another table.

"Get that fucker!" a voice shouted in English. The accent was unmistakably American.

The Israeli threw himself behind the next table and landed flat on the floor. A salvo of full-auto projectiles smashed into the table that Katz had chosen for cover. A bullet ricocheted off a nail head and struck a floorboard near Katz's rib cage. A familiar bolt of fear traveled up the Phoenix commander's spine; only a lunatic is not afraid when someone is shooting at him. Katz wondered if McCarter would have been frightened under the same circumstances.

Katz could only lie still and pray that none of the bullets struck home. He wondered what the hell had happened to Hahn. Had he fallen asleep or had they already killed him?

Karl Hahn was awake and alive, but his situation was not much better than the Israeli's. The German commando's Walther had skidded under a table beyond Hahn's reach. The only weapon he had left was the tiny .25 Bauer automatic, useless except at extremely close range.

The enemy fire seemed to be directed exclusively toward Katz's position. Hahn decided to try for the fallen P-5 pistol. He carefully crawled forward and eased around the corner of the table. A large-caliber bullet smashed into the floorboards less than an inch from the BND agent's outstretched fingers. Hahn hastily retreated as a pistol bellowed again. A big slug chipped wood from the table leg.

"Scheisser," Hahn rasped as he rolled on his left side to draw the .25 Bauer from his pocket.

The German crawled under the table, his arm extended with the diminutive pistol in his fist. Hahn slowly moved toward the advancing gunman. If he could get close enough, he thought he would be able to take out an attacker with the Bauer and get his hands on a real weapon. Of course, there was a good chance that he would get himself killed, instead, but he had never counted on dying of old age. In Hahn's opinion, a bullet in the heart or brain was better than most forms of death by natural causes.

Hahn continued to low-crawl under the table. He reached the end nearest to the aggressors. Less than a yard separated him from the next table, but if Hahn tried to crawl to new cover he would become a perfect target for the enemy. He would be totally exposed to enemy fire and completely helpless. The BND man took a deep breath and prepared to make his move.

Something moved under the next table. A startled pale face stared at Hahn. The assassin cursed under his breath and pointed a big .45 Colt 1911A1 pistol at Hahn.

The German ace snap-aimed his Bauer and squeezed the trigger as fast as he could. The distance between the BND commando and his opponent was less than two yards. They were close enough to spit on each other. Yet Hahn aimed at the gunman's face and missed.

The trigger man screamed when a .25 caliber slug split the third knuckle of his index finger. Bone and cartilage burst apart and the digit was torn from its base. The killer could not fire his Colt in response. His trigger finger was gone. Blood spat from the jagged stump and splattered the slide section of the .45 pistol.

Hahn fired the .25 twice more. A bullet pierced the back of the assassin's hand. The small, low-velocity projectile burrowed into skin and muscle and lodged in the center of the man's palm. The Colt fell from his bloodied, trembling hand. The third round smashed into the gunman's face. Bone splintered in the man's cheek and his head recoiled from the blow.

The German agent squeezed the trigger of his Bauer once more. The fourth .25 caliber missile sizzled into the gunman's open mouth. It bit into the roof of his mouth and split the bone of the upper jaw. Tiny shards were driven high into the brain. The gunman convulsed briefly as life quickly slipped away.

The amplified hee-haw of a German police siren announced the arrival of the Munich *Polizei*. A pair of officers entered the beer hall. Both carried Heckler & Koch service pistols in their fists.

"Donnerwetter dochmol!" a voice exclaimed.

Two enemy gunmen suddenly leaped onto tables and opened fire with their automatic weapons. Parabellum slugs crashed into the two policemen. Bullets ripped into their chests and kicked their bloodied bodies backward. One cop fell against a window, smashing both the glass and framework. His corpse tumbled through and smacked against the pavement.

Yakov Katzenelenbogen took advantage of the distraction. He aimed his SIG-Sauer autoloader around the edge of the table. The front sight of the P-226 found the upper torso of one of the gunmen. Katz squeezed the trigger. A 9 mm round punched into the killer's chest and drilled into his heart.

The impact of the parabellum spun the man around. Katz fired two more rounds. Both 9 mm slugs struck the gunsel between the shoulder blades. He uttered a choked groan and fell forward, tumbling from the table. His body hit the floor like a mishandled side of beef.

The other gunman had already jumped from his table and was trying to aim his Walther MPL submachine gun at Katz. He did not notice Karl Hahn as the German agent rolled from cover and aimed his Bauer at the assassin.

The little .25 auto barked twice. One round stabbed into the gunman's lower intestine. The other bullet caught him between the legs. The projectile tore into his left testicle and tunneled upward. The man shrieked and triggered his Walther chatterbox.

Nine millimeter slugs sprayed the beer hall as the wounded gunman blindly fired his MPL. Hahn and Katz remained behind cover as the bullets smashed into furniture and walls. Unfortunately one of the tavern customers chose that moment to raise his head. Two 9 mm slugs shattered his forehead and blasted through brain matter to the back of his skull. The man died before he even heard the shots that killed him.

The wounded trigger man fell against a table, the Walther subgun still in his grasp. Hahn moved from his cover and aimed the Bauer at his opponent. He squeezed the trigger. Nothing happened. The little .25 was out of ammo. Hahn swore under his breath, annoyed with himself for not bringing a spare magazine for the Bauer. He discarded the .25 auto and got to his feet, pulling a bench from under the table with him.

Hahn picked up the bench and held it in the middle. The wounded gunman was doubled up, one hand clawing at his maimed genitals, while the other still held the Walther MPL. The gunman glanced up as Hahn charged; the German agent was using the bench as a battering ram.

The assailant tried to raise his weapon, but he was not quick enough. Hahn lunged forward, driving the end of the bench into his opponent's chest. A corner of the bench struck the killer's solar plexus. The powerful blow lifted the man off his feet and pitched him backward. The machine gun fell from his grasp and clattered across the tabletop as the hoodlum slumped to the floor.

Katz advanced cautiously, scanning the area for other attackers who might still be lurking within the beer hall. He moved toward the original trio of assailants. Two were obviously dead. The third man was curled in a ball, both hands clasped to his gut-shot lower abdomen.

The Israeli knelt by the terrorist. The man did not appear to be breathing. Katz could not check for a pulse with the metal fingers of his prosthesis, so he was forced to return his P-226 pistol to shoulder leather. He lowered his prosthetic hand next to the man's head as he holstered the SIG-Sauer. Katz then pulled the glove off his left hand with his teeth and placed two fingers to the man's neck. The carotid artery throbbed beneath his skin.

Suddenly the wounded terrorist rolled on his back. He held a compact Hi-Standard derringer in his blood-soaked hands. A twisted smile crossed his pain-racked features as he pointed the tiny two-shot pistol at Katzenelenbogen.

A .22 slug crashed into the hoodlum's left temple. The high velocity projectile punctured his brain and blasted an exit hole at the opposite side of his skull. Katz swept the derringer out of the man's grasp with the back of his left hand. The gunman's body twitched weakly as Death quickly claimed another victim.

Katz glanced at the gray smoke that curled from the end of his right index finger. The artificial digit was actually the steel barrel of a single-shot pistol that had been built into the prosthesis. The tip of the glove around the finger had been split open by the .22 round. The muzzle of the small gun barrel was visible through the gap.

"Well," Katz said with a sigh. "There goes another pair of gloves."

5

"I hope you people appreciate that you've created a real mess for us," Harold Farrel complained as he paced the floor of the conference room. "Ten people killed, including two Munich police officers, a member of the Czechoslovakian Embassy and an innocent bystander. That sort of thing doesn't improve Uncle Sam's image in this part of the world."

"Sorry," Yakov Katzenelenbogen said dryly. "I'm afraid that when people are trying to kill me, I tend to forget that defending myself can often be taken out of context by the media."

"Shame on you," David McCarter said with exaggerated alarm. "Didn't you realize that it would have caused far less trouble if you'd simply let those blokes kill you? Selfish bugger. Of course, it might not have looked so good if *both* Czech officials had been killed instead of only one."

"No one would have been killed if you men had acted properly," Gert Ulrich declared sharply. "This is the Federal Republic of Germany, not the American Wild West. We don't condone gunfights in the streets of our cities."

"And the United States government doesn't like being connected to this sort of behavior, either," Farrel added.

Farrel was a case officer for the Central Intelligence Agency. A small wiry man with a nasal voice, he wore single-breasted suits, skinny striped ties and white shirts with starched collars. The CIA man looked like a minor-level bureaucrat, and that was exactly what he was.

Gert Ulrich, the BND control officer, resembled a professional mourner. His thick body was clad in a black three-piece suit complete with a black tie. His black derby sat on the table near his elbow. The corners of his mouth seemed to be locked in a downward position and his eyes were solemn and brooding.

Katz and Hahn had met Farrel and Ulrich almost immediately after the firefight in Munich. An ambulance had taken Matus Meret to a hospital and the police had briefly questioned Katz and Hahn about the shooting. However, the BND and CIA were waiting for them at the police station. The cops reluctantly released Katz and Hahn to the feds.

They soon found themselves at the conference table in a soundproof meeting room at BND headquarters. The other members of Phoenix Force were already present. The BND had rounded them up earlier that evening while Katz and Hahn were meeting their contact at the Wagner Beer Hall.

"I don't know who you people are or how you managed to get White House approval," Farrel stated. "But I don't like the way you operate."

"Who gives a shit what you like, fella," Calvin James replied with a yawn.

"We could have you arrested and deported from the Federal Republic as undesirables," Ulrich declared.

"I'm a German citizen," Hahn said with a shrug. "Where would you deport me to?"

"You're also a member of the BND," Ulrich snapped. "We'll take care of you later."

"Spare us your threats," Gary Manning told him. "You have a situation on your hands that is far more 'undesirable' than we are. You should be more concerned with who sent a hit team to the Wagner Beer Hall and why they did it."

"If Warburg and Hahn hadn't killed all the attackers," Farrel complained, "perhaps we'd know who sent them."

"I tried to take one of them alive," Hahn said with a sigh. "I only hit him with a bench, but the blow stopped his heart. I tried standard CPR techniques, but he was already dead."

"The claim that dead men tell no tales isn't always true," Manning said with a shrug. "We should be able to identify the attackers. They have faces, fingerprints, teeth that can be checked against dental records if we can get some leads on the bastards."

"One thing is already certain," Katz stated. "At least one of them was an American."

"What?" Farrel glared at the Israeli. "Are you sure?"

"I'm certain," Katz said with a nod.

"Now that's interesting," Ulrich began, turning toward Farrel. "Isn't it?"

"Why are you looking at me that way?" the CIA man demanded. "You don't think the Company is responsible for this, do you?"

"The CIA has been involved in assassination plots in the past," Ulrich declared. "Even a former CIA director admitted that your organization once considered having Castro killed."

"Considered," Farrel said, jabbing a finger at Ulrich. "That doesn't mean the Company ever agreed to actually carry out any assassinations, and it certainly doesn't mean we'd kill two Czech diplomats."

"But if you *were* planning to kill two Czech officials, you wouldn't want to kill them on American soil, would you?" Ulrich snickered.

"All right," Katz said sharply. "This has gone far enough. I wasn't suggesting that the CIA was responsible for the incident at the Wagner Beer Hall. I wish you'd let me explain. Whoever sent those assassins is probably linked to the terrorist activity in Czechoslovakia that Meret and Kohout told us about.''

"You don't know that for certain," Ulrich stated, turning his frosty gaze on Karl Hahn. "I seem to recall that Herr Hahn has made a lot of enemies among the Red Army Faction and the Baader-Meinhof gang. That's why the GSG-9 got rid of you, isn't it? Some sort of personal vendetta, correct?''

"My best friend was killed by terrorists," Hahn explained. "No, 'killed' isn't the right term. They weren't that generous. The bastards castrated Klaus and gouged his eyes out of their sockets. He was still alive when I found him. They had him strapped to an armchair with piano wire. Blood covered him like a layer of red paint. Have you ever smelled that much blood? Have you ever looked into the face of a close friend and seen nothing but agony and mutilation?''

"You killed him," Ulrich stated. "Shot him at the base of the skull.''

"That's right," Hahn admitted. "What would you have done, Herr Ulrich? Left him like that? Tried to keep him alive so they could sew him together and help him adjust to a new life as a blind eunuch?''

"I wouldn't have sought revenge by hunting down and slaughtering terrorists," the BND control officer declared. "Did you think you were Charles Bronson in one of those terrible American movies? It's a wonder the BND accepted you after that vigilante nonsense.''

"I only killed terrorists," Hahn said with a shrug. "And I didn't torture them as they did Klaus. I simply executed the lice.''

"Executed?" Ulrich glared at him. "My apologies to Mr. Bronson. You think more like Mack Bolan.''

"Thank you for the compliment," Hahn replied with a smile.

"Let's stay on the subject," Katz insisted. "The gunmen at the Wagner Beer Hall were definitely hunting Meret and Kohout. Karl and I just happened to be at the right place at the wrong time."

"How can you be so sure?" Farrel demanded.

"Have you ever heard of the German Red Army Faction or the Baader-Meinhof gang working with American fanatics in Western Europe?" Katz asked. "Also, both the Red Army and the Baader-Meinhof gang are Marxist organizations that almost always carry Soviet- or Czech-made weapons. The gunmen at the beer hall were armed with West German and American weapons."

"That isn't proof." The CIA man clucked his tongue with disgust.

"Why are we wasting time talking to these blokes?" David McCarter asked angrily. "Didn't anyone tell these deskbound paper pushers that we're in charge?"

"There's obviously been a communications problem," Katz stated. "Probably due to bureaucratic fumbling. The CIA and BND probably couldn't get their act together when they tried to cross-check information and coordinate who to send as their respective representatives."

"Fumbling?" Ulrich raised his eyebrows. "That fumbling is called 'security precaution.' We didn't intend to charge into this the way you did...."

"Which is why neither the BND nor the CIA had anyone at the hall to contact us when we met with the Czechs," Katz cut him off sharply. "In this business, you have to know the difference between being foolhardy and being decisive, and between using reasonable caution for security purposes and failing to do your job because you're afraid to act promptly."

"Shit on 'em, man," James announced. "Let's have these jerks pulled from the mission and get somebody we can work with."

"What do you mean?" Farrel asked.

"Check your instructions," Manning said. "You'll find that you're supposed to take orders from us, not the other way around."

"I hope that won't be necessary," Katz said. "Herr Ulrich and Mr. Farrel were selected because they're professionals. They're among the best liaison officers in Western Europe and we'd have a hard time getting suitable replacements. We need well-placed contacts within the CIA and BND for this mission." Katz continued as he turned to Farrel and Ulrich, "Your experience and connections within the espionage community will be very valuable to us."

McCarter rolled his eyes. James scratched an eyebrow to conceal a smile and Manning nodded in silent agreement. They understood why their commander was trying to mend fences with the CIA and BND officials. Phoenix Force did need contacts within the two intelligence networks and getting new liaison officers would take up valuable time. Katz was willing to do a bit of ego stroking if it meant that Farrel and Ulrich would cooperate with them.

"Well," Farrel began, "we're all on the same side. What do you want us to do, Mr. Warburg?"

"We need more information from Meret," Katz replied. "More details about what's happening in Czechoslovakia. Obviously we can't get that sort of information from the Czech government. We'll also need information from your intelligence sources. Find out what the rumors are on the underground."

"Naturally," Ulrich confirmed. "How badly is Meret injured?"

"Not critically," Katz assured him. "Meret will be able to talk, but we have to make certain he doesn't talk to anyone besides us."

"No problem," Ulrich promised. "What else do you need?"

"Information about the attackers," Manning supplied the answer. "There's usually a lot of documentation on both Americans and West Germans. If the Americans entered the country legally, and if they haven't had cosmetic surgery or drastic alterations to their fingerprints and teeth, it shouldn't be too difficult to find out who they are. Of course, all German nationals over the age of sixteen are required to have a passport. They should be even easier to track down."

"We'll see what we can come up with," Ulrich replied. "Hahn, you're a computer expert. Do you want access to our records department?"

"That would be very helpful," Hahn answered.

"The same goes for access to CIA computers at the American Embassy," Farrel added.

"I'll also need access to Interpol and to the division of the NSA that is stationed in the Federal Republic," Hahn announced.

"NSA?" Farrel said, wrinkling his nose as if he smelled something putrid and loathsome.

The National Security Agency is the largest American intelligence network, much larger than the CIA, although few Americans know of its existence. The NSA specializes in gathering information from surveillance sources around the world. The rivalry between the CIA and NSA is somewhat less than friendly.

"And access to U.S. Army intelligence," Hahn continued. "Also, the BfV should be contacted and a computer linkup established."

"BfV?" Ulrich groaned.

The Bundesamt fur Verfassungschutz is the West German equivalent of the FBI. The BND and the BFV are as compatible as the CIA and the NSA.

"The BfV has the most complete set of criminal records relating to West German offenders," Hahn explained. "Since some of the men who attacked us were Germans, it's probable they've had some sort of trouble with the law in the past. The BND generally doesn't keep the records of common criminals unless we feel they're connected with the terrorists or enemy espionage activities. The BfV might be able to help. If they don't have anything, we can go through them to contact Interpol and local police departments."

"In the meantime," Katz began, "someone will have to contact the Czech Embassy and tell them about Meret and Kohout."

"What?" Farrel glared at the Israeli. "Are you serious?"

"Ten people were killed in a gun battle in Munich," Katz replied. "How long can you keep a story like that out of the papers? The Czechs will find out about it, anyway. It'll be better for our interests if they hear it from us first. Of course, there's no need to tell them everything. Keep in mind that Meret and Kohout met with us because they needed help, and they didn't sound as though they were representing the Czech government or the Soviets."

"In other words," McCarter added, "those chaps deserve a cover story that will protect them from retribution. Kohout is dead, but his family could still suffer if the Reds think he was a traitor. If you sell them out just to have an easy political scapegoat, I will personally see to it that you regret that decision."

"Is that a threat?" Farrel demanded.

"It's a bloody warning," the Briton replied. "I don't usually give a man a warning. I generally just figure out who the enemy is and put a bullet through his head."

"Take it easy, St. John," Katz urged, referring to McCarter by his current cover name. "These gentlemen aren't our enemies."

"Just making conversation," the Briton said with a shrug.

"Terrific," Farrel muttered, wondering what asylum they had sprung McCarter from. "Do you guys need anything else?"

"About six gallons of coffee," James replied. "This is going to be a long night."

"And some Coca-Cola," David McCarter added quickly. "That is, if you've got the *real* Coca-Cola, not that so-called New Coke, which tastes like watered-down paint thinner."

"Did you know that if you put a human tooth in a glass of Coca-Cola it'll dissolve in less than seventy-two hours?" Gary Manning commented. "Ever think of what that stuff does to your stomach?"

"I don't have teeth in my stomach, mate," the Briton answered simply.

EIGHT HOURS LATER Phoenix Force had some answers, as well as some new questions. The computer investigation had identified all six men who had launched the attack on the Wagner Beer Hall. Four attackers had been German nationals and the other two were American citizens.

The German gunmen all had a history of criminal behavior that ranged from creating a public disturbance to assault. They had been young men in their early twenties, products of middle-class families with strictly white Teutonic ancestry. Most important, all had been members of the United German National Party.

A small, very militant right-wing organization, the UGNP had been under surveillance by the BfV, the NSA and several police departments since it's first public appearance three years earlier. The UGNP was staunchly anti-

Communist and it endorsed severing all diplomatic relations with the Soviet Union and its satellite nations. They wanted to unite West and East Germany under a single flag—a popular concept among many Germans on both sides of the Berlin wall. However, this idea was not very popular with most other Europeans or Americans. The vision of a powerful united Germany resurrected images of Hitler's minions. There was evidence that most Soviets were equally apprehensive about this notion—which was not surprising when one considered that more than a million Russian soldiers had been killed during World War II.

The UGNP favored an increase of NATO defense forces in Germany and an escalation of sophisticated hardware for the Germany military. The party was also an outspoken critic of Israel, which it blamed for driving Arab nations into alliance with the Soviet Union. The UGNP frequently linked Judaism with Communism. Critics tended to label the UGNP a "neo-Nazi" organization, something that made modern Germans extremely uncomfortable.

Although the UGNP had been under scrutiny by the authorities, the radical group had never been definitely linked with any violence more extreme than an occasional fist fight with members of the left-wing, antinuke Green Party. The UGNP had been considered more of a nuisance than a threat—until now.

The information on the American gunmen was equally as surprising. The late George Jennings and Harvey Lindon had entered West Germany three months before the incident at the Wagner Beer Hall. Both had used genuine passports and claimed to be tourists. Thanks to Interpol computers and a telecommunications satellite linkup with the FBI, the investigation uncovered some intriguing facts about the two Americans.

Jennings had been a member of the American Nazi Party. He had a criminal record that included a conviction for armed assault and the illegal modification of a firearm—he had converted a semiautomatic weapon to full auto. Jennings had also been suspected of being connected with the kidnapping and murder of a leftist college professor who openly endorsed Marxism.

Harvey Lindon had also been a jailbird; he had spent three years in the Maryland State Penn for manslaughter. He had killed a black man during a barroom brawl. Witnesses testified that the fight had occurred after Lindon had made abusive racist remarks. He became a member of the Aryan Brotherhood while behind bars, and may have participated in acts of violence against nonwhite inmates. Of course, none of these suspicions was ever confirmed.

The main link between the two Americans was the fact that both Jennings and Lindon had joined the World Army Freedom Network. WAFN was a paramilitary organization founded by Zackery Briggs, a wealthy and outspoken right-wing political activist.

The self-proclaimed "Colonel" Briggs was no stranger to the American media. His extremist views received more press coverage than they deserved. Briggs had advocated the use of nuclear weapons on numerous occasions. At various times he had wanted to nuke Cuba, Red China, North Vietnam, Iran, Libya and, most of all, the Soviet Union.

Briggs was the millionaire son of Harold Briggs, a noted industrialist and stock-market wizard. He had used his family inheritance to create WAFN, an organization that many critics believed was modeled on Hitler's Waffen-SS.

"Sounds as though the United German National Party and WAFN are birds of a feather," Calvin James commented after hearing the results of Karl Hahn's investigation.

"Indeed," the German agent agreed as he leafed through another manila folder. "Of course, neither organization is illegal, but both have been suspected of being involved in various criminal activities.''

"Which either means they're innocent or very careful,'' Gary Manning mused as he poured himself a cup of coffee.

"We'd better assume the latter,'' David McCarter advised, sipping from a can of Coca-Cola Classic.

"Well,'' Hahn began, "the two organizations are definitely connected. Almost a hundred members of WAFN have been slipping into the Federal Republic for over a year. They enter the country as tourists and never leave.''

"Any idea where they are?'' Katzenelenbogen inquired.

"Many of them appear to be staying at the home of Klaus Weiss.''

"*The* Klaus Weiss?'' Manning asked. "As in Weiss Manufacturing?''

"That's right,'' Hahn confirmed. "One of the top producers of industrial machinery and tools in the world. Weiss is listed among the ten wealthiest men in the Federal Republic. Like Briggs, Weiss is an outspoken opponent of Communism, leftist liberals and Zionism—whatever that is.''

"Depends on who you talk to,'' Katz said.

"Weiss is the biggest supporter of the UGNP,'' Hahn added. "Some say he's the real leader of the party, although Herman Drache is the official head of the United German National Party.''

"Drache.'' McCarter frowned. "That name sounds familiar.''

"I'm not surprised,'' Hahn answered. "Drache was something of a national embarrassment to my country a while back. He was in England at the time, connected with the British chapter of the Ku Klux Klan.''

"The KKK in England?'' Calvin James said with surprise.

"Unfortunately." McCarter sighed. "The Klan isn't very large in Britain, but it's there."

"Drache was trying to stir up the Klan," Hahn explained. "Trying to convince its members to commit acts of violence against the Soviet Embassy in London, Jewish citizens, that sort of thing. The British deported Drache and sent him back to Germany. He's been the darling of the UGNP ever since."

"No accounting for taste," Manning said with a shrug. "Why do you think the WAFN is staying with Weiss?"

"Well, they aren't all at the Weiss estate," Hahn stated. "But Colonel Briggs is among his house guests."

"Briggs is here?" Katz raised an eyebrow. "Now that is interesting. Any idea what he's doing here?"

"The BfV and the BND didn't have any reason to be interested in their activities until now," Hahn answered. "After all, there's nothing illegal about having house guests, and frankly, the authorities are not eager to pry into the personal affairs of Klaus Weiss. He has friends in parliament and many connections within the international trade and banking communities. He's not the sort of man any government agency wants to upset."

"It's so much easier to harass low-income individuals, instead," James commented dryly. "Figure we ought to see what these fellas are up to?"

"Sounds like a capital idea to me," McCarter replied.

"Thanks for volunteering," Katz told the Briton. "Karl is the natural choice to look into this business and you can accompany him."

"Lucky me," Hahn muttered, well aware that McCarter was the unit crazy.

"Check with the BfV and BND for any info they might have on Weiss," Katz urged. "We don't want to step on the toes of any of our allies."

"Right," Hahn agreed.

"Remember, this is a recon mission," Katz added, largely for McCarter's benefit. "We want information, not a large body count."

"We could try for both," the Briton said cheerfully.

"David . . ." Katz began sternly.

"Just kidding, mate," McCarter assured him.

"Uh-huh," Manning muttered suspiciously.

"I hope so, David," Katz said with a sigh.

6

Klaus Weiss owned a large estate in Bavaria. His property covered fifty square miles, although much of the land was forest. A small narrow road ran through the woods adjacent to the Weiss estate. A tall wire fence surrounded the extent of the property. A sign, written in German, English and French, was posted at regular intervals to warn that trespassers would be "dealt with harshly."

A Volkswagen Golf cruised along the otherwise deserted road. McCarter, Hahn and two BND agents rode in the car. It traveled at a casual pace until the driver found a wide area at the shoulder of the road. The VW rolled onto the shoulder and came to a halt.

"Das ist es," Hanaes Brauner, the BND agent behind the wheel, announced. He translated his remark for McCarter's sake. "This is the place, *Meine Herren*."

"Weiss doesn't encourage visitors," Albert Schwalb added. The second BND agent sat in the front seat next to Brauner. "We've done very little spying on this place. Some time ago we were ordered to look the place over, but not to do anything that might upset Weiss. The situation is a sensitive one."

"So we heard," McCarter remarked as he took a pack of Player's cigarettes from his pocket. "I'm surprised you blokes even found out that Briggs was staying here."

"Wasn't easy," Schwalb admitted.

"We won't see a damn thing from here," Karl Hahn said as he opened one of the doors and slid out of the VW.

"Unless you want to trespass," Brauner began, "the best way to get a look at the place is to climb a tree. You should see the back of his home from this point."

"Climb a tree, eh?" McCarter muttered. "I just hope we aren't barking up the wrong one."

"Let's find out," Hahn suggested, handing the Briton a pair of Bushnell binoculars.

The four men walked to the base of a large pine tree. McCarter pulled up the zipper of his dark-green windbreaker and slipped on a pair of leather gloves. All four men wore jackets. The autumn weather was brisk and the wind carried a sharp chill. The garments also concealed the pistols they carried in shoulder leather just in case trouble occurred.

The British ace slipped his head through the neck strap of the binoculars and then reached for the closest branch. McCarter hauled himself up the tree, bracing his feet against the trunk. He easily found hand and footholds as he climbed higher. The Phoenix pro reached a fork of two thick limbs about thirty feet from the ground. He wedged himself between the limbs and raised the binoculars to his eyes.

The Bushnells allowed McCarter to peer through a gap between treetops on the Weiss estate. Although McCarter's view was limited, it was obvious that the wealthy manufacturer owned a large mansion. The architecture appeared to be a strange mix of European Gothic and Beverly Hills. The ornate cornice and roof cresting reflected the former style. A picture window and marble patio at the rear of the house looked like the typical Hollywood set. Weiss even had a kidney-shaped pool, although no one would use it at that time of year unless they belonged to the Polar Bear Society.

Sudden movement caught the Briton's attention. A jeep rolled along a paved driveway that passed the house. Two men rode in the vehicle. The driver and his companion were both dressed in dark uniforms with caps and shoulder patches. Security patrol, McCarter thought. It was hardly surprising that Weiss would have his own guard force to protect his property. McCarter was sure that one of the patrolmen was armed with an H&K G-3 assault rifle. No doubt Weiss had made certain that his guards had government permits to carry full-auto weapons.

McCarter followed the jeep through the lenses of his Bushnells. The vehicle headed toward a collection of buildings to the west. The Briton whistled softly when he saw them.

Two buildings were long and very plain one-story structures. A smaller, two-story building stood facing the billets. Several trucks and jeeps were parked at the end of a parade field. McCarter had seen hundreds of military barracks in the past and he had no doubt that he was looking at another one. Weiss and Briggs had constructed a miniature paramilitary base on the estate. The barracks even had a name. A sign read Fort Odin Two.

"Can you see anything?" Hahn called up to him.

"A bit," the Briton replied, scanning the area to see if he had missed anything.

McCarter climbed down from the tree and reported his findings to the three Germans. Brauner and Schwalb were shocked by the news. The barracks had not existed when they had done their last recon.

"You two obviously know more about what's going on in there than we do," Brauner told McCarter and Hahn. "Do you mind filling us in?"

"What's the significance of 'Fort Odin Two'?" Schwalb asked.

"Probably a sequel to Odin One," McCarter said with a shrug.

"Maybe it has greater meaning," Brauner said, raising an eyebrow. "I seem to recall that *odin* is a Russian word."

"Oh-deen," Hahn corrected. "It means one. But I don't think we need to pursue that line of thought. Mr. St. John certainly would have told us if the sign were in Cyrillic letters."

"Hell," McCarter replied. "I wouldn't have been able to read it. The sign was in plain English. I'd say 'Odin' refers to the emperor of the gods in Norse mythology. Viking gods have always been a favorite among warriors."

"Is that important for any other reason?" Schwalb wondered.

"Perhaps," Hahn said grimly. "Norse mythology has often blended with Teutonic legends. Some of Hitler's prize racists, such as Himmler and Haushaufer, were believers in a type of quasi-mysticism in which Odin was the great white warrior god of the Aryan people."

"Scheisser," Brauner rasped. "Let's not jump to any conclusions. God knows, we don't need to remind the world of what Hitler and his butchers did."

"The world can't afford to forget, either," McCarter stated.

"It won't," Brauner assured him. "People still talk about the six million who were killed in Hitler's death camps, although little is said about the thirty million slaughtered during Stalin's reign or the more than sixty million murdered by Mao Tse-tung. How much is said about the Siberian labor camps that still exist today? People would rather drag up Hitler's ghost and condemn Germany for what happened forty years ago."

"I don't fully understand that double standard," Hahn remarked. "As a German born after the war, I also find this frustrating. Perhaps Nazism is more readily condemned than Communism because there were so many photographs and so much film footage taken at the concentration camps after the Allies liberated the prisoners. There have been few photos taken of Siberian camps, and certainly none as dramatic as those of Auschwitz, Buchenwald or Dachau."

"But the Russians are constantly committing acts of oppression and aggression," Schwalb stated. "They invaded Afghanistan in 1978 and they're still occupying the country, fighting Afghan rebels opposed to Communism. Yet people seem far more upset by American involvement in Vietnam. The Russians shot down a 747 commercial airliner and killed more than two hundred innocent people, but that's been largely forgotten."

"Not forgotten," McCarter stated. "It just isn't popular to discuss such things. People are frightened by the possibility of a nuclear war. The governments of the West have been trying to establish treaties with the East. Nobody wants to rock the political boat by accusing the Soviets of violating agreements."

"Do you think the Communists are responsible for whatever Weiss and Briggs are up to?" Brauner asked with a frown.

"That certainly wouldn't fit their public image," Schwalb commented. "Of course, the whole thing could be an elaborate cover."

"We don't know any more about this than you do," Hahn assured him. "And I don't think we'll learn much standing around here. Let's see if we can get a better look at the estate from a different angle."

Brauner fished the car keys from his pocket and headed toward the VW. The other men followed as the driver opened the car door and prepared to slide behind the wheel. Suddenly he groaned and fell backward. The sharp report of a rifle echoed from the forest. Brauner's body twitched slightly as blood bubbled from a large hole in his chest.

"Gutt Gott!" Schwalb exclaimed, pulling his H&K 9 mm pistol from its shoulder leather.

McCarter and Hahn had already drawn their weapons and ducked behind the cover of the VW Golf. They scanned the area, searching for the sniper. The muffled roar of an engine announced the presence of another vehicle in the forest. It was the jeep with the two Weiss security patrolmen. One held a bolt-action rifle with a telescopic mount. He worked the bolt to eject a spent cartridge and then chambered a fresh round. The driver steered the jeep straight for the VW.

"Schweinhunden!" Schwalb shouted as he fired his Heckler & Koch at the advancing vehicle.

"Hold your fire!" McCarter snapped. "They're way out of pistol range!"

Hahn repeated the command in German to make certain that Schwalb understood. McCarter knelt by Brauner's body. The Phoenix pro checked for a pulse although he was certain Brauner was already dead. After confirming his fear, the Briton pulled the car keys from the dead man's grasp and scrambled inside the car.

A large-caliber bullet slammed into the open car door. It punched through metal as though it were plywood. The projectile sizzled past McCarter's left arm, missing the limb by less than an inch. The Briton barely noticed. He was too busy trying to start the car.

Hahn yanked open a door and dived into the back seat. He was followed by a visibly shaken Schwalb. The Briton tried a key in the ignition. It did not fit. He inserted another key.

A bullet struck the windshield. The projectile hit at an angle and ricocheted off the curved surface of reinforced safety glass. A crack appeared, but the glass held. McCarter turned the key and the engine groaned. The monotonous putter sounded like a mechanical dirge as the car refused to start.

"Bloody hell," McCarter growled, pumping the gas pedal. He tried the key again.

The engine roared to life.

"Schnell!" Schwalb urged desperately.

"Shut up and keep your head down," McCarter growled as he shifted the gears to drive.

The VW bolted forward and shot up the road. The enemy jeep rolled across the forest in pursuit. The driver paid more attention to keeping track of the Golf than of his immediate surroundings. He had to slam on the brakes to avoid crashing headlong into a tree.

"They stopped," Hahn announced, peering out the back window. "The idiot nearly wrecked the jeep."

"A pity they didn't both go through the bloody windscreen," McCarter commented as he continued to floor the gas pedal.

"Here's another pity for you," Hahn stated. "One of the bastards appears to be speaking into a walkie-talkie."

"Which means we can expect more company," McCarter groaned.

The accuracy of the Briton's prediction soon became apparent. A second jeep carrying Weiss security rolled onto the road, about four hundred yards in front of the Volkswagen. The jeep aimed at the Golf and charged.

"What do we do now?" Schwalb demanded, the H&K pistol trembling in his shaky hands.

"Keep your bloody head down, damn it," McCarter insisted. "Karl, are we ready for some music?"

Hahn opened a briefcase and removed an H&K MP-5 machine pistol. He jacked a 9 mm parabellum round into the chamber and switched off the safety catch.

"I've tuned up my instrument," he announced.

"Then we're ready for the concert," the Briton said with a wolfish grin.

McCarter met the enemy's charge, driving the VW straight toward his opponent. The driver of the second jeep accepted the challenge and kept coming. His companion aimed an assault rifle at the Golf and opened fire. McCarter hunched low as high-velocity projectiles smashed into the cracked windshield. Glass burst, sending several shards inside the VW. Schwalb cried out as a sharp sliver slashed his cheek.

"Told you to keep your head down," McCarter reprimanded his passenger as he shook his head to toss chunks of broken glass from his hair.

The Volkswagen and the jeep continued to race toward each other in a deadly game of chicken. The patrol car did not flinch from the likelihood of a head-on collision. The driver plunged toward the Golf while his partner fired another burst of full-auto rounds at the Golf. The distance between them closed rapidly. Three hundred yards. Two hundred. One hundred . . .

McCarter suddenly turned the wheel sharply to the left. The VW spun in a wide arch, dust flying from the tires and brakes screeching as the Briton fought to keep the car from going out of control. The jeep was less than ten yards away. The driver tried to swerve around the Golf as he tried to avoid a crash and offer his gunner the best available target.

Karl Hahn poked the barrel of his MP-5 through the back window and opened fire. A volley of 9 mm slugs chopped into the torso of the enemy gunman. The multiple bullets lifted him out of his scat and hurled the patrolman backward over the side of the jeep. He fell from the open vehicle and crashed to the ground in a lifeless heap.

The jeep's driver stomped on the accelerator. Hahn trained his Heckler & Koch on the fleeing vehicle and sprayed the jeep with parabellums. Bullets racked the rear of the jeep. At least one punctured the gas tank. Others sparked against metal. The tank ignited and the jeep exploded into flames. The blast flipped the vehicle, burying the driver in the fiery wreckage.

McCarter pulled the VW away from the shoulder and pointed the car in the direction from which their opponent had come. The whine of a bullet that ricocheted across the trunk warned them that the first jeep was back on their trail—and that the sniper with the scoped rifle had not run out of ammo.

"The roads in this country are bloody awful," McCarter complained as he stomped on the gas pedal.

The Golf shot across the road, moving deeper into the Black Forest. Hahn could barely see the general shape of the pursuing jeep. But that was enough. The sniper rifle had far more range than a machine pistol. The enemy did not need to be beside the Golf to be effective.

"Gott im Himmel!" Schwalb exclaimed. "We will never get out of here alive!"

"What's the matter?" McCarter sneered. "Don't you have insurance, mate?"

"The forest is getting denser up ahead," Hahn noted as he swapped magazines for the MP-5. "If the enemy doesn't get too close, we might be able to slow down without them seeing us. Then we can set up an ambush."

"It's not likely we'll lose them," McCarter replied as a low hanging branch scraped the roof. "Those blokes know this area better than we do."

"Then how can we outrun them?" Schwalb demanded. "That jeep is better suited to this sort of terrain than our car. They'll catch up with us in a matter of minutes."

"Unless you have a useful suggestion," the Briton said crossly, "will you just shut up and keep your head—"

A bullet shattered the glass in a rear side window. The projectile hissed past Hahn's ear, making the hairs on his neck stiffen. Schwalb's head bobbed violently as the lethal messenger smashed into the back of his skull. Blood and brains were sprayed over the car's interior. Schwalb's body slumped to the floor without uttering a sound.

"Maybe now you'll keep your head down," McCarter muttered.

"I wonder about you sometimes, David," Hahn whispered, unnerved by the Briton's attitude.

"I'll send flowers later," McCarter replied gruffly. "Right now there are other things to worry about."

The road extended up a hill. Tree branches brushed the Volkswagen as the car climbed higher. The enemy jeep was still trailing them but was getting gradually closer. The patrolmen knew they had the advantage as they realized that the odds were in their favor. As long as they stayed out of pistol range, they could simply pick off their targets one at a time.

"Take the wheel," McCarter told Hahn as he reached for the handle to the car door.

"What?" Hahn stared at the Briton.

"Reach over here and take the bloody wheel," McCarter insisted. "I've got an idea."

"Oh, no," Hahn said with a sigh, familiar with the Briton's knack for reckless action.

"Just do it," McCarter said as he opened the door.

Hahn reached across the backrest and grabbed the steering wheel. McCarter slid out from under the wheel, grabbing the open door to haul himself outside. The German commando cursed softly as he awkwardly steered the car, his body draped over the backrest.

"Isn't this taking back-seat driving a bit too literally?" Hahn commented through clenched teeth.

McCarter did not bother to reply. He was too busy trying to pull himself up onto the top of the car. A tree branch swatted the Briton's arm, nearly knocking his hand away from the door. Pine needles stung his cheek and one narrowly missed an eye. McCarter placed a hand on the car roof to brace himself as the Volkswagen began to slow down.

"Drive the son of a bitch, Karl!" McCarter shouted.

Hahn climbed into the front seat and sat behind the wheel. He pressed a foot to the accelerator, urging the car toward the summit of the hill. McCarter braced a foot against the door handle and raised an arm to brush aside the branches. The Briton saw his chance, and without hesitating, he reached for a thick branch. McCarter knew that if he missed he would probably lose his life.

The Briton's left hand struck the limb. Propelled by the motion of the speeding VW, McCarter's palm hit hard. The impact caused his hand to bounce off the surface, but McCarter's fingers clawed at the bark and held on. His other hand quickly grabbed the branch as his feet swung free of the car door. McCarter kicked his legs forward and hooked an ankle on the limb.

The Volkswagen continued to race away from the tree. Hahn drove it over the summit and headed the car down the opposite side of the hill. McCarter wrapped both legs around the tree limb and held on with his left hand. His right reached inside his jacket to draw the Browning Hi-Power autoloader from shoulder leather.

McCarter had little time to prepare for action. The pursuing jeep appeared at the summit. The driver's eyes were trained on the windshield, seeking the Volkswagen. The rifleman held his weapon in combat readiness as he also searched for the fleeing car. Neither man noticed McCarter in the tree above them.

The British warrior snap-aimed his Browning and opened fire. His first 9 mm round punched the rifleman in the center of the chest. The sniper convulsed when the hot metal tore into his flesh. His eyes revealed more surprise than pain.

McCarter pumped another parabellum into the sniper's chest and quickly shifted the Browning toward the driver.

The jeep was still moving. The driver did not slow down when he heard the shots. He barely flinched when his rifle-toting partner slumped dead in the seat beside him. The guy kept his foot on the gas pedal, but he could not get far enough fast enough. McCarter fired two quick rounds that struck the driver between the shoulder blades.

The Phoenix pro watched the jeep swerve off the road as the wounded driver fell sideways, turning the wheel sharply. The vehicle crashed head-on into a tree trunk. Metal crumbled from the impact, glass burst from the windshield and the bodies of the two patrolmen were tossed from the Jeep as though they were a pair of blood-laced rag dolls. McCarter jumped down from the tree and cautiously approached the still bodies. He did not think either man could have survived. He was right.

Satisfied, the Briton returned his Browning to its shoulder holster.

7

Sentries stared down at the mechanical rhinos rolling toward the gates of the Weiss estate. Machine guns were mounted on the three armored cars and each vehicle was equipped with a 40 mm cannon. Two military trucks followed the steel-plated cars. The trucks transported the troops: GSG-9 antiterrorist commandos and paratroopers from the 449 Airborne Battalion of the West German defense force.

Hahn and McCarter had reported the incident at the Weiss estate to the other members of Phoenix Force. The BND was informed of the shooting that had claimed the lives of two of their agents. Three hours later the GSG-9 and the German paratroopers were called into action.

The five men of Phoenix Force were among the assault force. Yakov Katzenelenbogen rode in an armored car with Colonel Ludwig Bohler, the GSG-9 commander. Katz and Bohler were old friends. The German colonel had worked with Phoenix Force to combat a deadly conspiracy organized by the ODESSA Nazis and a splinter group of the Baader-Meinhof gang. The GSG-9 colonel knew few details about the mysterious and elite strike force that Katz commanded, but he realized it was one of the world's most highly skilled antiterrorist teams.

"They're opening the gates," Bohler noticed. "Either these characters don't plan to put up a struggle, or they intend to lure us into a trap."

"Better assume the latter," Katz advised. "I'm sure your men know to watch for land mines and other booby traps."

"*Ja,*" Bohler said with a nod. "Our biggest worry is that the enemy might have heat-seeking missiles. Of course, if they fire one missile, our forces will use our rocket launchers to blow them to pieces. The mortar teams are posted beyond the fences of the property. By the way, what should I call you these days?"

"'Warburg,'" Katz said with a smile. Bohler was one of the few men who knew the Israeli's true identity.

"All right, Warburg," Bohler replied. "I see you have Karl Hahn on your team. He used to be one of my men, you know."

"That's why we're confident he's a professional," Katz confirmed.

"Professional, *ja,*" Bohler began, peering through a porthole as the armored car rolled across the threshold of the Weiss estate. "But Hahn is a bit of a maverick...that is the English term, *ja*? I'm sure you know about his vendetta."

"I know about it," Katz assured him.

"Does not worry you, eh?" Bohler laughed. "Well, what is one more crazy person in your group? I remember a tall Japanese and a tough Hispanic figher. I hope they were not killed in action."

"They're elsewhere," Katz replied simply. He trusted Bohler more than he trusted most men, but there was no point in telling him of the fate of Keio Ohara or Rafael Encizo. The less Katz told him, the less chance of an accidental security leak.

"I see," Bohler replied. "The black man seems competent. Of course, you wouldn't have him on the team if he were not."

"Mr. Walker is highly professional," the Israeli said, using Calvin James's current cover name.

"Never hurts to have another reliable man in circumstances such as these," the GSG-9 officer commented.

James and Hahn were stationed with the troops outside the Weiss property. They would watch for escape attempts and supply backup to the main assault force if needed. Manning and McCarter were with the troops in the trucks to coordinate ground forces within the estate if a battle erupted.

However, as the vehicles rolled along the paved drive toward the Weiss mansion, not a single patrolman working for the manufacturing magnate offered any resistance. The guards stood next to their jeeps, unarmed and hands in plain view. Other security personnel were in a military formation, standing at parade rest. None appeared to be armed.

"Looks like Weiss doesn't want to fight," Bohler mused.

"Maybe not," Katz agreed, picking up his Uzi submachine gun. "But let's not jump to any conclusions. Things are not always as they seem."

"I'm going to instruct my men to round up the security people and hold them at gunpoint," Bohler stated. The tall, blond colonel took a Walther P-38 from a hip holster and worked the slide to chamber a round. "Do you want to come with me to pay Herr Weiss a visit?"

"I'd be delighted to accompany you," Katz replied.

The first armored car, containing Katz, Bohler and three GSG-9 commandos, stopped in front of the mansion. The other two armored vehicles headed for the rear of the house. One of the transport trucks followed. They were more concerned about an attack from the men stationed at Fort Odin Two than from the men in the mansion. GSG-9 commandos and paratroopers poured out of the other truck. Troops covered the security guards while others hurried to join Katz and Bohler as they emerged from the armored car.

"I received a radio message from Walker," Gary Manning announced as he approached the two colonels. "He reports that there has been no sign of activity at Fort Odin. It looks like a ghost town back there. And no one has tried to escape since our men moved into position."

"So far this raid has been about as exciting as invading Dinkelsbühl," Bohler remarked.

"That's rather strange," Katz mused as he scanned the stained-glass windows of the mansion. "Klaus Weiss has gone to great lengths to protect his property, yet his people haven't even made a rude gesture. Four of his guards attacked some of our people just for peeking over the fence, and now they're as docile as sheep."

"Maybe they don't like the odds," Bohler suggested. "We've got more than a hundred men and a lot of firepower. If they initiate a confrontation, we're ready to fight back hard."

"Yeah," Manning replied as he unslung his Remington shotgun from his shoulder. "Or maybe they want to choose the time and place for battle. But let's not assume too much in either case."

He snapped the SWAT-style folding stock into place and checked to be certain that the shotgun was in the safety mode. The Canadian propped the Remington blaster under his elbow, pointing the muzzle at the ground as he walked toward the mansion. Katz and Bohler followed suit. No one wanted to overreact, and yet they knew they had to remain cautious.

They mounted the stairs to the open doors. A flashbulb exploded as they approached the threshold. A small, swarthy man with a pencil-thin black mustache lowered a Minolta camera and smiled at the three commandos. His grin vanished when he realized that all three men had automatically aimed their weapons at the flashbulb. The photographer retreated as the trio stepped to the doorway.

"Kommen sie heir," a voice invited. "Come here. You wanted to see me, so enter."

The voice belonged to a middle-aged man who sat in a thronelike armchair. Anyone familiar with the members of the European establishment would recognize Klaus Weiss instantly. His bushy gray eyebrows and long, thick sideburns were a stark contrast to his high forehead and receding hairline. The businessman's eyes were dark and stern, his mouth a hard line and his nose a small knob in the center of his face.

Weiss sat in the center of an enormous, yet sparsely furnished hall. The floor was solid marble. Only two paintings hung on the wall, although a blank space suggested that a third had recently been removed. Katz noticed that one painting depicted a sword-wielding figure on horseback. The other was of a stern figure dressed in royal uniform. The paintings were of Charlemagne, the Holy Crusader from Aachen, and Otto von Bismarck, the first chancellor of Germany.

Katz realized the importance of these two historical figures. The Nazis believed that Charlemagne's reign was the First Reich and that Bismarck's rule marked the Second Reich. Katz had no doubt that the missing painting was of Adolf Hitler, the ruler of the Third Reich.

"I am Frederick Grimm," a portly man dressed in a three-piece, pin-stripe suit announced as he stepped from behind Weiss's chair. "Herr Weiss's personal attorney. May I see your search warrant, *bitte*?"

"We don't need a search warrant," Colonel Bohler replied. "Surely you are familiar with the National Antiterrorist Act. If the police or government authorities have valid reason to suspect that a person or persons are involved in terrorism, then the need for a search warrant can be waived."

"Terrorism?" Grimm glared at Boher. "That is an outrageous accusation! Herr Weiss is a respected industrial leader, not only in the Federal Republic of Germany, but throughout the world. Just because you're policemen, or soldiers, or whatever, it doesn't give you the right to harass innocent people.''

"And we have a proof," the photographer added, his German thickly accented with a Venetian flavor. He raised the camera to snap another photo.

"It seems you were expecting visitors, Herr Weiss," Katz said, turning his head just before the flashbulb popped. The Israeli had developed a sixth sense for avoiding cameras. The sensation of eyes sighting in on him had always made Katz flinch, a trait that had prevented any government security agency from acquiring a recent photograph of the veteran commando.

"Why do you say that?" Weiss inquired.

"The response by your security force, the presence of your lawyer and this shutterbug suggest as much," Gary Manning commented.

"My attorney is here to advise me about handling an unfortunate incident that happened just outside my property. Some of my security personnel were involved," Weiss stated. "Vito Rossi is my personal photographer. His work is world famous, you know. Naturally I invited him here to take photos of the wreckage."

"That wreckage includes the bodies of two BND agents who were murdered by your security guards," Bohler said sternly.

"There are signs warning against trespassing," Grimm declared. "Herr Weiss has a legal right to protect his property. His guards are legally authorized to carry automatic weapons while on duty at this estate...."

"The BND agents were killed *outside* the estate," Katz said. "And we have witnesses who will testify to that fact."

"I'm aware this happened," Weiss admitted. "I have already called the police and reported the incident. The patrolmen involved were new men, young and overly zealous.

They were also killed. Did your witnesses happen to see who did it?''

"Of course," Katz answered. "They killed your men in self-defense.''

"That is their story," Grimm said with a shrug. "Don't most killers claim they acted in self-defense?''

"You're the lawyer," Manning replied. "You tell us.''

Vito Rossi raised his camera and snapped another photo. Manning turned and smiled thinly at the photographer. Katz clucked his tongue in annoyance.

"What right did the BND have to watch my client?'' Grimm demanded. "Without probable cause, this sort of harassment is not justified. It is indeed regrettable that an agent for the BND should be killed in the line of duty because his superiors ordered him to commit an illegal act. The Nazis have been gone for a long time, gentlemen. Your gestapo tactics are no longer tolerated in the Federal Republic of Germany...."

"If you want to take us to court, that's your privilege," Bohler announced. "However, we have reason to believe that you're giving assistance to terrorists and may in fact have established a base for training terrorists. I believe it is called 'Fort Odin.'''

"Fort Odin?'' Weiss repeated with a chuckle. "So that's what this is about. Come along, gentlemen. I'll show you Fort Odin and you can do all the searching you want.''

"We appreciate your cooperation, Herr Weiss," Colonel Bohler replied, taking a walkie-talkie from his belt. He switched the button to Transmit.

"What are you doing?'' Grimm demanded.

Bohler ignored him as he spoke into the radio. "Captain Weber, do you read me?''

"Ja, Mein Herr," a voice replied from the walkie-talkie.

"Gut," Bohler said. "I want you to take thirty men and search those billets in Fort Odin Two. If you find anyone back there, hold them until I say otherwise."

"I understand, Colonel," Weber assured him.

"And watch yourselves," Bohler warned. "If anyone resists, do what you have to. Shoot to kill, if necessary. If you encounter an organized resistance, blow the barracks to hell."

"Jawol," the captain replied.

"Zair gut," Bohler said as he ended the transmission. "Now, Herr Weiss, while my men search Fort Odin, we will look around your house. Any objections?"

"Of course I object," Weiss told him. "But under the circumstances, I have no choice but to allow you to search my home. I shall save my objections for the courtroom, where I shall see you gentlemen again . . . defending yourselves and your organizations against a lawsuit."

"We'll worry about that later," Bohler stated.

Katz realized that the GSG-9 commander did not feel as confident as he tried to sound. Weiss was too calm, too smug. If the manufacturer was connected with terrorism, he had disposed of any and all incriminating evidence. More than four hours had passed between the gun battle outside the estate and the raid. Not much time to pull up stakes and run, but it was more than enough time for a disciplined military unit that was trained to travel light and that was prepared to move at a moment's notice.

The search confirmed Katz's fears. They completed a grand tour of the main floor of the Weiss mansion without finding anything that could link the tycoon to any kind of terrorist activity. Weiss and his lawyer escorted the three commandos through the hall to an enormous dining room. The furniture was hand-rubbed oak. A crystal chandelier hung from the center of an intricate display of sword-wielding cherubims and bluish flames that were painted on the ceiling.

The kitchen was equipped with all of the modern gadgets and conveniences of twentieth-century culinary art. It also had a large refrigerator, two stoves and a walk-in meat freezer. The den contained a large leather-top teakwood bar with columns of glass shelves stocked with expensive liquors. The stuffed heads of big-game animals from Africa, Asia and North America were displayed at strategic positions around the room. Firearms filled a great glass case. The weapons ranged from a British elephant gun to a Schmeisser MP-40.

"Would you like to see the upstairs now?" Weiss inquired as calmly as a real-estate agent showing a house to a prospective buyer.

"Let's see the basement first," Katz replied.

"The basement is unsafe," Grimm said quickly. "It's undergoing some repair work...."

"We're brave," Manning assured him. "We'll take that chance."

"All right," Weiss replied with a shrug.

"Herr Weiss," Grimm began, "as your attorney, I feel—"

"I feel you should be quiet before these gentlemen become impatient," Weiss said sharply. "I've got nothing to hide down here. In fact, I'll be interested in hearing what they think of the decor."

The "decor" of the basement was indeed unique. A wooden rack with freshly oiled manacles occupied the center of the room. Chains and torture instruments designed to remove noses and ears hung from the wall. An iron maiden sat in one corner. The shape of this ancient device of mutilation and murder resembled a full-figured woman. The maiden opened like a pair of closet doors. The interior of the device was lined with dozens of sharp steel spikes.

"Welcome to my 'black museum,' as the British would say," Weiss said with a chuckle.

"This is your recreation room, Herr Weiss?" Manning asked. He tilted his head toward the rack. "Or just a place for guests to stretch out for a while?"

Rossi's flashbulb popped as he took another photo of the three visitors. Grimm snapped angrily at the photographer. "Don't take pictures down here, you fool!" the attorney warned.

"Relax, Frederick," Weiss said. "I should explain that I've been trying to collect various types of artifacts that reflect the Germany of the past. Unfortunately torture has always been part of European culture."

"These torture devices are in good condition," Katz commented, examining an assortment of whips that hung from a wall.

"I try to keep all of my belongings in good condition," Weiss replied.

"This iron maiden has steel spikes that appear to be machine made," Gary Manning remarked as he peered inside the ghastly contraption. "I didn't know they had that sort of technology during the Inquisition."

"Of course they didn't have anything like that during the Middle Ages," Weiss admitted. "That maiden was probably made sometime in the nineteenth century. It is very unlikely that the iron maiden was ever used during the Inquisition or that it even existed at that time, except perhaps in the minds of imaginative storytellers."

"A major campaign during the Inquisition involved obtaining confessions of heresy and witchcraft," Katz mused. "I wouldn't imagine they'd have much use for a device that stabbed a victim with numerous spikes simultaneously."

"Exactly," Weiss agreed. "Oh, there was supposedly an authentic iron maiden at Burg Castle, but the place was destroyed by bombs in 1945. However, a former director of the

Nuremberg National Museum believed that the maiden in the castle was a nineteenth-century fake. Most of the torture chambers in European castles are forgeries, recently added to impress the tourists who expect a medieval and macabre atmosphere.''

"You get many tourists, Herr Weiss?" Manning inquired.

"The torture chamber will be part of a Germanic museum that will be built in the future," Weiss explained. "Of course, my museum will recognize that the iron maiden is a hoax, as is the pit and the pendulum on display in a number of dungeons in Europe. There's not a single historical case involving such a device. Edgar Allan Poe, the American author, made it up for his story about the Inquisition."

"Will your torture chamber include any tools of the trade used by the Nazis in their concentration camps?" Katz asked, a hard edge creeping into his voice.

"Well, some of those whips were used by SS guards to drive prisoners through the gates of Dachau," Weiss announced with a smile. "I also have a set of surgical instruments used for experiments on Jews and other prisoners. These even include a pair of pliers that were probably used to pull out gold teeth from the mouths of Jewish merchants whose days of gouging the German public had ended. Speaking of gouging, there's also a device that resembles a pointed spoon. I suspect it was used to scoop out eyeballs in order to study the optic nerve of a living person."

"I've heard stories of such things," Katz said, his voice barely above a whisper, his eyes as hard as marbles.

"I think we'd better inspect the rest of the house now," Colonel Bohler suggested, worried that Katz might become upset and decide to exercise his frustrations on Weiss.

The rest of the tour was uneventful. Although the torture chamber was bizarre, it was not illegal. Katz, Manning and Bohler failed to find anything to link Weiss with ter-

·orism. A radio report from Captain Weber confirmed the ṣuspicion that Fort Odin Two was deserted.

"I hope you're satisfied," Frederick Grimm told the trio as they headed toward the front door. "You've harassed an ḥonest pillar of the community with this illegal search. I inṭend to see to it that you regret this day."

"Where's Zackery Briggs?" Katz asked, ignoring Grimm ẹnd directing his question to Klaus Weiss.

"Herr Briggs is my guest, not my prisoner," Weiss reạlied. "He is free to come and go as he wishes."

"And so are all his friends," Manning commented. "What's Fort Odin? Is that Briggs's idea?"

"The original Fort Odin was Briggs's idea," Weiss coṇirmed. "It's in the United States. Texas, I believe. Briggs ạnd I decided to build a second Fort Odin here. We're ṭraining patriots opposed to Communism so they'll be able ṭo defend themselves if the Soviet Union attacks. There's ṇothing wrong with that, is there? Unless, of course, you ḥappen to be a Communist."

"There's nothing wrong with preparing to defend yourṣelf against any sort of threat," Katz assured him. "As long ạs your methods don't endanger the lives of innocent peoḍle."

"I assure you, we're very careful," Weiss stated. "And all ẉeapons used here are kept under lock and key except for ṭhose for training purposes and those carried by the guards ḟor security reasons. All are legally licensed with the govḙrnment, of course."

"Since you gentlemen could not find anything to subṣtantiate your accusations," Grimm began, "you are now ṭrespassers on private property. I suggest you leave immeḍiately before the charges against you increase."

"We're going," Bohler replied with a sigh.

Vito Rossi's camera popped another flashbulb. Without ẉarning, Manning's hand streaked out and yanked the camera from the photographer. The Canadian smiled at Rossi as he opened the back of the camera.

"What do you think you're doing?" Grimm demanded. "You have no right to—"

"Just want to be certain Mr. Rossi didn't photograph something that might prove to be important evidence concerning terrorist activity," Manning answered.

"Give me back that camera!" Rossi cried.

Manning pulled the film from the camera in order to expose it. Satisfied that the film had been ruined, the Canadian tossed the Minolta to Rossi.

"Sure," he said, discarding the film. "Didn't find any evidence, anyway. Thanks for letting me check it out, fella."

"Come on," Bohler urged. "Let's get out of here."

8

"Congratulations," Harold Farrel began dryly. "Your raid was a total disaster."

"I don't know about that," Gary Manning replied. "We saw a nifty torture chamber and I learned more about the iron maiden than I ever wanted to know."

"That isn't amusing," the CIA case officer complained, drumming his fingers on the table in the conference room. "Do you realize what a scandal this business could cause?"

"I don't see why that should concern the Company," Gert Ulrich said angrily. "Two of my agents were killed, not your men."

"If Weiss carries through with a lawsuit," Katz began, taking a pack of Camels from his pocket, "it will be directed at the GSG-9, and not at the BND or the CIA. Of course, Weiss will probably try to settle out of court. That will involve your agency, Herr Ulrich. Weiss will want the BND to agree that everyone's best interests would be served by simply forgetting the whole incident."

"Forgetting?" Ulrich glared at the Israeli.

"Weiss is one of the most powerful men in the Federal Republic," Karl Hahn stated. "But even he can't simply dismiss the fact that two BND operatives were murdered by members of his security force. He'll probably decide that his men overreacted when they attacked us. Of course, Weiss will be certain to point out that the guilty patrolmen have already paid for their crime with their lives. I think Mr.

Warburg is right. Weiss will be willing to forgive and forget the raid on his premises if we agree to sweep everything else under the rug."

"The sad thing is that's probably the best thing we can do for our own sake right now," Farrel muttered.

"The hell with Weiss," Calvin James announced. "Right now, he's not important. We should be worrying about Zackery Briggs."

"But you did not find Briggs at the estate," Ulrich said.

"No, we didn't," James agreed. "But we did find a lot of tire tracks, and judging from the indentations in the ground, those vehicles were heavy. They were probably loaded with men and equipment. Briggs is on the loose with an army. He's bound to figure that somebody will be watching the Weiss estate for a while, so he won't head back there. Trouble is, what will he decide to do while he's on the run?"

"I've got a theory about that," David McCarter began. "Those blokes fled the area pretty damn quickly. That means they must have been on standby, ready to pull out at a moment's notice. They were already prepared before we had our little donnybrook with the security guards. That means they were getting ready for a mission. Whatever it is, it has to be something big."

"You have no proof," Ulrich frowned. "That's pure conjecture on your part."

"Briggs didn't send over a hundred members of his World Army Freedom Network to Germany on a European vacation," Katz remarked. "He didn't build Fort Odin Two because he was bored. The attack on Meret and Kohout at the beer hall links the WAFN and the United German National Party with the terrorism in Czechoslovakia."

"Not necessarily," Farrel said. "There may be no connection at all."

"We don't have the sort of proof that would stand up in a court of law," McCarter said with a shrug. "But we've still got enough circumstantial evidence to be ninety-eight percent certain that the WAFN and the UGNP are the culprits.''

"So you think we should search all of Germany and hunt down Briggs and his crew?'' Ulrich sighed. "Even if we find them, we can only bring them in for questioning . . . unless you plan to take matters into your own hands again, Hahn.''

"I wouldn't do that,'' Hahn replied. "Not as long as there's a two percent chance that we might be wrong.''

Ulrich stared at Hahn, uncertain whether he was joking. Katz decided to cut into the conversation before tempers flared.

"Finding out who's behind the terrorism in Czechoslovakia is our primary concern,'' the Israeli announced. "If what Meret tells us is accurate, the acts of violence against Soviet personnel in Czechoslovakia aren't really upsetting the Soviets, but they will almost certainly escalate the Soviet presence in Czechoslovakia. The Czechs won't like that, and neither will we. If the KGB thinks that the CIA and BND are responsible for these killings, it won't be long before the Russians start to retaliate. The KGB believes in revenge and the Morkkrie Dela assassins are very good at their job.''

"It's already started,'' Farrel said grimly.

Ulrich stared at him reproachfully. The CIA man ignored him.

"Want to tell us what happened?'' James inquired.

"One of our people was murdered last night,'' Farrel answered. "A woman in the records department. Just a secretary with a security clearance. At first we thought it was a heart attack, but an autopsy found traces of cyanide on the hairs inside her nostrils.''

"A poison-gas pen,'' Katz mused. "A favorite method of assassination among KGB hit men.''

"Another operative was killed by a hit-and-run driver in Bonn," the CIA officer continued. "The police found the car that hit the guy. It belonged to a German national who's only prior arrest was for drunk driving. The owner was in the car, passed out with a lump on his head. A blood test determined that he had been drinking, but the guy claims he was struck from behind and framed. Naturally nobody believes him."

"That might not be the work of the KGB," Ulrich stated.

"Maybe," Farrel replied. "But my sources tell me an NSA agent also had a fatal heart attack this morning and that one of your people had a nasty accident. He fell in the shower and broke his neck, right?"

"If you wish to discuss classified material concerning the CIA, that's your business," Ulrich snapped. "But I don't appreciate your talking about BND matters, Mr. Farrel."

"It's hardly a state secret," the CIA officer said. "I think we'd better be more concerned with our survival than in trying to keep secrets from each other. Hell, Gert. You or I might be next on the KGB hit parade."

"Is there any way we can contact the KGB and try to arrange a truce?" Katz inquired.

"Truce?" Ulrich raised his eyebrows. "You can't be serious. How can we establish a truce with the Russians when we're not responsible for the assassinations in Czechoslovakia? We have nothing to bargain with."

"Try to explain our theory about the right-wing terrorists," Manning suggested. "Just contact the Soviet Embassy. Half their staff is KGB, anyway."

"Do you think the Russians will believe us?" Farrel asked.

"They might if we can show them some proof," Hahn began. "Airport security is very tight, especially after last year's bomb incident in Frankfurt. If any members of the UGNP or the WAFN have recently traveled to Czechoslovakia on legitimate flights we might be able to get the proof we need if we can get our hands on the videotapes from the airport surveillance cameras.''

"If we can identify any of the bastards," Farrel commented. "You know, the Soviets will still think we sent those lunatics."

"If the situation was reversed, we'd feel the same way," Manning mused. "Right now, all we have to do is try to convince the Soviets that we want to try to stop this mess before it gets any worse. If they want to think we're trying to call off our dogs, let 'em."

"That's like trying to put a Band-Aid on a bullet wound," Farrel said with a sigh. "That won't cure the problem. How do we solve it?"

"We'll have to go to Czechoslovakia," Katz answered. "The enemy's primary mission must be taking place there. Weiss is too clever to keep any incriminating materials at his home, if in fact he's been privy to the whole scheme. Briggs might take days to find, and even then there's not much we can do except deport him along with any of his followers that we discover. The real problem is in Czechoslovakia."

"And you think you can just stroll across the border and hunt down a bunch of lunatics that the KGB and the Czech STB haven't been able to get close to?" Ulrich inquired.

"Something like that," Manning answered.

"Oh?" Ulrich replied. "And do you also think the Soviets and the Czech government will welcome you with open arms and agree to help you in this quest?"

"No," Katz began. "I don't imagine they'll be very cooperative."

"Then how do you intend to deal with the Communists?" Farrel asked.

9

The Berlin Wall is the most famous and the most visible section of the iron curtain. Yet the barriers separating East and West extend from Hamburg to Vienna and from Hatzeburg to Bratislava. These barriers are not always brick walls or fences of cyclone wire. Some fences are simply barbed wire and posts. Sometimes innocent wanderers accidentally cross into Communist territory, mistaking a simple barrier for the fence of a farm or private forest. Many of these individuals are poachers who carry rifles or shotguns to stalk illegal game. Most of these trespassers are shot down by East German or Czech patrols before they realize their error.

Three trucks and a jeep lumbered through the Bavarian forest, carefully maneuvering between the trees along a path of flattened grass. The convoy approached a long stretch of barbed wire, one of the most vulnerable points in the iron curtain.

Zackery Briggs sat beside the driver of the jeep. The American wore a U.S. Army fatigue uniform with silver eagles pinned to his collar and cap.

Briggs smiled as he drew the cool autumn air into his lungs. The WAFN leader was pleased with how the mission had gone thus far. Beside him, Darrel Kelly, the baby-faced flunky who drove the jeep, was visibly trembling with fear. This would be Kelly's first time behind enemy lines. Briggs tried to understand Kelly's nervousness, but sympathy, compassion and empathy had never been among his dominant character traits. Briggs had never been frightened by combat, not even the first time he saw action in Korea. The self-proclaimed colonel had decided he was simply courageous by nature, and he realized that he would have to tolerate those lesser mortals who were subject to fear.

It never occurred to Briggs that a lack of fear in a dangerous situation might be irrational. Briggs was certain he was sane. In fact, he was convinced he was superior to most of his fellow human beings. Briggs always found a way to blame his mistakes and errors on others.

But he had not always been so confident of his infallibility. Zackery had grown up in the shadow of a millionaire father, terrified of the great responsibilities that he was to inherit. Young Briggs had never learned to relate to people. He was taught to manipulate, to plan and to take action. As a youth he was unpopular with his peers and shy with girls. His inferiority complex, combined with the ruthless creed of his industrialist father, steered the boy's personality toward egomania to compensate for his repressed fears and his sense of inadequacy.

Briggs joined the military in an effort to rebel against his father's plan for his future. Of course, any bright young man from a wealthy family was welcome at West Point. Briggs attacked the challenge with fanatic zeal. He did not earn the friendship of others, but gained their professional respect. Zackery Briggs preferred it that way.

His followers still respected and feared him. They trusted his leadership and obeyed him like well-trained guard dogs. Although his career in the United States Army ended in scandal, Briggs became a folk hero among the militant right. Briggs selected the most gung-ho members of this lunatic fringe for Fort Odin. Wealthy, influential and outspoken, Briggs soon gained a form of eccentric fame. He enjoyed the limelight and the power he wielded over others. Eventually it led to a desire for more power and influence, more recognition as a leader.

He justified his personal ambition with lofty claims of dedication to his country, devotion to world freedom and opposition to Communism. Colonel Briggs had been playing this role for so long he had convinced himself of his socalled beliefs. His grasp of reality and his judgment were clouded by the complex array of extremist notions and conflicting mental ghosts that haunted the rat's maze of his mind.

"Relax, Kelly," Briggs told his driver. "We've made it past the troops guarding the fence on this side. That worried me more than confronting the Commies on the other side."

"But the guys on this side are American soldiers," Kelly replied, unable to suppress a shiver although the chilly night wind had not penetrated the vehicle.

"Of course," Briggs agreed. "I don't mind killing Commies, but I wouldn't want to have to kill American servicemen who are just doing their job."

"No, sir," Kelly replied woodenly.

The WAFN colonel smiled as he recalled how easy it had been to bluff his way past the U.S. patrols near the border. Briggs had flashed his forged identification and ordered the soldiers to let him through immediately. They had responded to his commands without question, instantly obeying and standing aside for the alleged NATO Defenses Inspection Unit. The tactic might not have worked with the German border patrols, who were considerably more professional than most military units stationed near the Czech border. However, the American troops tended to be less cautious.

Briggs was not surprised. The condition of the United States armed forces distressed him. They lacked discipline and their training was too rushed, with more emphasis on drill and ceremony than combat and security. It was a peacetime army, he thought. An army without a war to fight is like a thoroughbred racehorse without a track to run. The military had gotten soft and weak. Well, that would change. Briggs would see to that.

The convoy drew closer to the fence. Colonel Briggs raised his arm for the other trucks to halt. Kelly applied the brakes and all four vehicles stopped in unison. Discipline, Briggs thought, delighted with his men's response. They were a team, a well-oiled fighting machine.

The men had trained for this night for months. The incident at the Weiss estate had forced them to go into action ahead of schedule, but everyone was ready and the mission was going smoothly. Men jumped from the trucks and assaulted the wire with metal cutters.

Riflemen, armed with silencer-equipped rifles and infrared scanners, covered the men at the wire. They watched the woods carefully, seeking any sign of Czech patrols or American border guards. The WAFN forces cut through the wire and Briggs signaled for the men to move out. They killed the headlights and every driver donned a set of Cat's Eye infrared goggles that transformed darkest night to mere dusk.

The convoy rolled across the border into Czechoslovakia. Briggs felt excitement pulse through his body; they were behind enemy lines. The mission had reached its first critical stage. An ordinary man might feel fear or apprehension, but Briggs was confident of his success. Everything was going according to plan, a plan that Briggs was certain God Himself smiled upon.

Two hundred yards from the first fence, the unit encountered a second barrier. The men with the wire cutters leaped from the trucks and hurried forward to clear the path once more. Without warning, an explosion burst from the ground near Briggs's jeep. He instinctively covered his head as clumps of dirt pounded the vehicle. Something stuck the hood and rolled against the windshield.

"Oh, Christ!" Kelly gasped, staring at the object.

It was a severed arm, the fingers still twitching in a bizarre muscle reflex that reminded the young American of a scene from a horror film. Briggs reached around to the windshield and pulled the gory arm from the hood.

"One of our men stepped on a mine," Briggs announced. The colonel grabbed a megaphone and shouted orders to his troops. "Everyone back to your vehicle! We're going to ram the fence!"

"But, Colonel," Kelly began. "We're in the middle of a mine field..."

"Step on it, Corporal," Briggs snapped, reaching for the silver-plated 1911A-1 Colt resting on his hip. "Do it now!"

Kelly obeyed. He had been trained to follow orders. He also knew that Briggs would not hesitate to kill him if he disobeyed a direct command during the assault. The jeep bolted forward and struck the fence; wire was pulled taut and two posts were uprooted. The jeep rolled across the barrier, followed by the three trucks. Incredibly not a single tire detonated a second mine.

"My God!" Kelly exclaimed. "We made it!"

"Of course," Briggs replied simply. "We must keep our eyes open. That explosion will probably attract some Commies. The bastards might not have the stomach for a fight, but we can't take any chances. We will wait here and dispose of them. We do not want them to warn their commanders of our arrival. Shoot to kill."

Two minutes later a pair of headlights cut through the shadows. A Czech border patrol jeep and a military truck hurried toward the site. The Czechs probably expected to find a small group of defectors, would-be refugees attempting to flee into West Germany. They would not be prepared for what confronted them.

Briggs's men had gotten out of their vehicles and had taken cover when the headlights were noticed. When the jeep was within range, half a dozen snipers opened fire. Sound suppressors reduced the report of their rifles to mere popping sounds, but the bullets drilled through the windshield of the Czech jeep and tore into human flesh. The driver and the officer beside him were killed instantly. The jeep swung out of control and crashed into a tree. Czech troops immediately leaped from the back of the truck.

A UGNP fanatic among Briggs's forces aimed a Heckler & Koch 69A-1 grenade launcher at the Czech truck. He fired a 40 mm explosive projectile at the target. The grenade erupted on impact, blasting the cab and the body of the truck into a flying collection of mangled metal and dismembered corpses. Flaming gasoline spewed across the wreckage and splashed across several bushes and trees. Two Czech soldiers shrieked as they staggered away from the blaze. Flames crackled and danced along their limbs and torsos. Fire ignited their hair and charred their faces.

Four or five members of Briggs's unit opened fire with automatic rifles and submachine guns. Bullets ripped into the burning figures, swiftly ending their torment. The flaming bodies tumbled to the ground.

"Don't waste ammunition!" Briggs snapped.

"We couldn't let them burn, sir," one of the gunmen replied, startled by his commander's callous attitude.

Automatic fire snarled from the west. Two of the WAFN and UGNP gunmen, who had participated in the mercy killing of the fiery Czechs, were abruptly dispatched to the next world by twin streams of 7.62 mm projectiles. Their bloodied bodies collapsed as Briggs's men returned fire.

Three Czech border patrolmen ducked behind the cover of tree trunks as bullets hailed down on their position. A fourth soldier was not as fortunate. He dropped his AKM assault rifle and fell to earth with four bullets in his chest.

Briggs took an M-26 fragmentation grenade from his belt and pulled the pin. He hurled the miniblaster toward the trees. The grenade exploded in the middle of a group of Czech troopers. The blast threw their bodies into the open. Briggs boldly drew his Colt pistol and charged. Several WAFN and UGNP gunmen eagerly followed his example.

A wounded Czech solider lay on his side. One arm hung by a torn strip of flesh as blood from severed arteries soaked his jacket. The crippled man gazed up at Briggs as the colonel aimed his pistol. Briggs triggered the weapon, pumping a .45 caliber round into the Czech's forehead.

The two other Czechs were probably already dead, but Briggs's followers double-checked by blasting their inert forms with 9 mm slugs. One of the gunmen stepped closer and kicked a dead Czech in the ribs. He turned to his comrades and smiled as he placed a boot on the corpse's rump. The killer held his Smith & Wesson chattergun against his hip, the barrel pointing toward the sky.

"Wish it wasn't so dark," he commented, his Boston accent clearly pronunciating every "s" as if it were the most important letter in the alphabet. "I'd sure like a picture for my scrapbook."

"Quit fooling around, Malloy," Briggs ordered. "Gather up the Czech's weapons and get back to the trucks. We have to get out of here."

"What about our dead?" Walter Cole, a captain in WAFN inquired. "We can't just leave them here."

"Toss them in the fire," Briggs replied, tilting his head toward the burning debris that had once been the Czech truck. "When we can afford the time, we'll give them a proper hero's funeral. Right now, we just have to get rid of them."

"Art was a Baptist," one of the troopers remarked. "I don't think he'd want to be cremated, sir."

"Then his ghost can haunt me later," Briggs snorted. "Burn them both."

The flames were rapidly spreading from tree to tree and fire was creeping across the grass in a steadily growing tide of burning destruction. Normally the WAFN and UGNP members would have tried to put out the fire before it destroyed the forest, but Briggs clearly intended to use the blaze as a diversion.

"Congratulations, men," Briggs announced. "We've won our first skirmish. You are now part of a battle-bloodied cadre. Now we've got a lot of work to do and we have to move fast. Chuck those bodies in the fire and let's move out."

10

Major Ladislav Svoboda jumped to attention when Captain Mikail Ivanovich Renkov entered the office. Although Svoboda was the senior officer, he was only a case officer with the Czechoslovakian Intelligence Service. Captain Renkov, however, belonged to the Komitet Gosurdarstvennoy Bezopasnosti. The KGB agent outranked the Czech intel officer as surely as the Soviet Union ruled the Czechoslovak Socialist Republic.

Svoboda was a well built, forty-two-year-old Bohemian who had been drafted into the STB during his stint in the miltary. Chosen for his intelligence and an aptitude for languages, Svoboda had been with the STB since 1970. Like many if not most Czechs, Svoboda was disillusioned with the Communist system that ruled his country. Yet he vividly recalled the Soviet invasion of 1968 and realized the danger of angering the great Russian Bear.

Mikail Renkov certainly did not resemble a bear. The KGB supervisor reminded Svoboda of a toad; the Soviet was a short, squat man with a flat Tatar face. Renkov's mouth was wide, with colorless lips and small blunt teeth. His nose was little more than a pair of nostrils, and his eyes had a slight Oriental slant. As a Tatar he had often been treated as a third-class citizen in the Soviet Union. Tatars and any other Turkic people living in eastern Russia have always been victims of considerable racial discrimination by both Russians and Ukrainians.

However, victims of prejudice do not always learn compassion and sympathy for others. Renkov had been accepted into the KGB because he was a devout Communist who had ruthlessly informed on members of his own family who had opposed the Kremlin. Renkov enjoyed both bullying the Czechoslovakians and exerting his authority over STB personnel such as Major Svoboda. Indeed, Renkov preferred to remain on assignment in Czechoslovakia, where he could be the oppressor instead of the oppressed.

"I'm glad to see you're in your office, Major," Renkov said with a sly grin. "I had feared that I'd have to wake you at this hour."

"Every military and law-enforcement officer in the country was alerted," Svoboda replied, placing a spoon in a cup before pouring hot tea. "I'm sure you heard what happened."

"Somebody broke through security at the border," Renkov stated. "A dozen or so soldiers were killed. Bold action, eh? Whoever did it wasn't too worried about causing an international incident or even triggering a nuclear war."

"It wasn't that serious," the Czech said as he stepped forward and handed the cup to the Soviet. The heavy scent of cheap lilac perfume assaulted Svoboda's nose as Renkov took the tea.

"It might be more serious than you imagine," the KGB man said, slowly stirring his tea. "You've been investigating this terrorist activity for some time. Still no idea where these bandits are hiding?"

"Not yet," Svoboda admitted. "Do you think there's a connection between the terrorists and the incident tonight at the border?"

"Perhaps," Renkov replied. "These terrorists are organized, you know. We've always assumed that the BND or the CIA was behind them, but now there's some evidence that suggests someone else might be involved. Someone perhaps worse than conventional intelligence agents.''

"Really?" Svoboda raised his narrow eyebrows as he lowered himself into the swivel chair behind his battered old desk.

"Da," the Soviet confirmed, sitting in an armchair across from the Czech officer. "KGB sources in West Germany have informed us that an elite international strike force is operating in Europe."

"Oh?" Svoboda gave him a blank stare. "Not the Baader-Meinhof gang, I trust."

Renkov stiffened. The Marxist Baader-Meinhof gang had been a tool of the KGB, carrying out acts of terrorism against the Federal Republic of Germany. They had been cannon fodder, unwitting pawns of the Kremlin's interest in disrupting the nations of the West.

"Hardly, Major," the Soviet said dryly. "I'm talking about at least five capitalist gangsters employed by the Americans. They may be of mixed nationality and they're comprised of different ethnic backgrounds. One is black. The other four are white. One of these is a middle-aged man with one hand or possibly an entire arm missing. A Canadian and a German have also been identified. The other man is simply described as being tall with quick reflexes. He is believed to be either American, English, Canadian or Australian."

"Are you certain we can rule out the Scots?" Svoboda asked.

"These men are extremely dangerous, Comrade," Renkov said grimly. "They've foiled several KGB operations in the past and they've killed at least a hundred Soviet citizens."

"A hundred?" The Czech's mouth opened with surprise. "Were these civilians?"

"Every citizen of the Soviet Union is a comrade," the KGB agent declared. "We are all equal under Communism."

"Spare me the quotations from *Pravda*," Svoboda insisted. "If these supercommandos have crashed through the border into my country, I would appreciate knowing some details. Did they slaughter civilians, or did they kill Soviet soldiers or agents in actual combat? Are they just butchers or fighting men?"

"I . . . don't know too many details, Major," Renkov admitted, obviously uncomfortable about the subject under discussion. "No one knows all the details involved. Yet I can tell you that these men were considered to be of such a threat that Moscow ordered them to be liquidated. An incredible unit was sent to the United States to deal with the gangsters. KGB, GRU from military intelligence and some of the best paratroopers in the Soviet army were assigned to the task."

"How many men?" the Czech asked.

"I'm not sure," Renkov said with a sigh. "Moscow doesn't dwell on such a failure and an embarrassment. I've heard that the strike force was more than a hundred men. Perhaps as many as two hundred."

"Two hundred trained agents, Morkkrie Dela assassins and paratroopers were defeated by five men?" Svoboda was stunned.

"Officially, no," the Soviet answered. "That traitor Burov was in charge of the unit. He defected to the Americans, you know. Moscow claims he probably undermined the entire operation from the start."

"Is that possible?" the STB agent asked.

"Anything is possible," Renkov said. "But it is unlikely. Burov probably defected because he realized he would be shot if he returned to Russia. I had a cousin, Vladamir Renkov, who worked with Burov. Vladamir told me that the bastard was a cold-blooded opportunist. By the way, my cousin was sent to America as a surveillance expert on the mission. He did not return."

"I'm sorry, Captain," Svoboda said. "These gangsters, as you call them . . ."

"And what would you call them?" the KGB agent demanded

"Professionals," Svoboda replied. "Let's not underestimate our enemy, Comrade Captain. That can be a fatal mistake. We Czechs learned that the hard way."

"I assume you're talking about the days when the Holy Roman Empire ruled your country," Renkov remarked. "Or perhaps when the Nazis seized control during the war."

"Of course," the STB agent agreed. "But let's just concentrate on these five capitalist swine. What are they? Espionage agents? Commandos? Mercenary soldiers?"

"Perhaps all three," Renkov answered. "It does not matter what they call themselves. They must be regarded as a serious threat. And it is possible that these five are the leaders of a much larger group."

"If they are the men who did in fact break through the wire," Svoboda replied. "But why would they charge in so abruptly and attract so much attention? Wouldn't such men enter the country discreetly?"

"They are ruthless and care nothing of human life," the KGB man stated.

"If they're as good as you say they are," the Czech began, "I'm certain they temper ruthlessness with professional caution. Crashing that fence was the act of bold and arrogant men. Did you know they drove those trucks across a mine field? One of their men was splattered all over the forest. Tire tracks were found over a mine that failed to explode."

"Pity." Renkov sighed. "It would have been convenient if the mines had taken care of the capitalist pigs."

"What bothers me most, Comrade, is why they brought in those trucks," Svoboda stated. "It can't be just to transport personnel. What did they transport into the country?"

"Weapons, explosives," the KGB officer said with a shrug. "Something like that. At any rate, you've been investigating the terrorism for some time. Now you'll also be looking for the American gangsters. Of course, your comrades in the KGB will be working with you and helping you, just as close brothers help one another through trying times."

"That's very reassuring," Svoboda said, trying to sound sincere.

"I knew you'd feel that way, Comrade Major," Renkov said with a thin smile. He consulted his watch and sighed. "Two o'clock. I really must get some sleep. I trust you'll examine the situation more closely and have a complete report ready for me by ten?"

"Of course, Captain," Svoboda assured him. "Pleasant dreams."

ALEXEI CERNAK RESEMBLED a bear as he crouched and duck-walked under the low roof of the tunnel. Dirt spilled from the rotting beams that supported the secret passage. He shook some of the dust from his shaggy black beard and glanced over his shoulder at the five men of Phoenix Force.

"Everybody still in one piece?" he asked, his English containing a thick Slovak accent.

The flashlight in Cernak's ham-sized fist illuminated his craggy face. Light reflected off a steel tooth as he smiled at his disgruntled companions. "Don't worry. It's not much farther."

"That's what you said half an hour ago," David McCarter complained. The British warrior hated closed-in areas and the tunnel was a claustrophobic nightmare.

"Half an hour isn't so long," Cernak replied. "We're that much closer now. But we're almost there. I make this trip between Czechoslovakia and West Germany five or six times a year. I know when we're getting close, eh?"

"I certainly hope so," Gary Manning muttered. For once, the Canadian and his British colleague were in agreement about something. Neither of the warriors enjoyed creeping through the dark, narrow shaft.

"Karl has made this trip with me a couple of times," Cernak declared. "Surely he told you that this route would take longer than other paths to Czechoslovakia. But it is the best way to enter the country without attracting the attention of the goddamn Communists."

Hahn had told the others about Cernak. The burly Czech had been opposed to Communism since the Soviet invasion of 1968. He and a group of resistance fighters had started to dig the tunnel when he was still a teenager. They were amateurs and experienced many problems building the shaft. Getting the necessary tools and materials had not been easy, and they had to work without drawing the attention of STB and KGB informers.

They worked for more than two years to complete the tunnel. A cave-in killed one of the resistance members and broke the leg of another. Yet they continued the project until it was finished. Cernak and four companions entered West Germany in 1973 and officially defected.

The Gunther Geion scandal of 1974 revealed how vulnerable the Federal Republic was to infiltration by enemy agents. Geion had been a top aide to Chancellor Willy Brandt. The discovery that Geion was actually a mole working for the East Germans had led to Brandt's resignation. Cernak and the other Czech refugees decided to keep their tunnel a secret from the authorities partially because of this scandal. They used the shaft as an "underground railroad," helping other Czechs escape from Communist oppression.

However, smuggling refugees was often a dangerous activity. Two of Cernak's friends were killed in a gun battle with the STB at a train station in Moravia. The other two decided to retire from the refugee trade. One moved to Switzerland and the other immigrated to the United States. Only Alexei Cernak remained to help fellow Czechs find the "midnight express" to freedom.

Although very brave and bold, Cernak was also a careful man and was extremely suspicious of West German intelligence, which has an alarming number of East German SSD moles. The 1985 scandal involving Hans Tiedge and his defection to the East was evidence that such concerns were not unfounded. However, Cernak trusted Karl Hahn to keep the tunnel a secret.

Hahn and Cernak had used the covert passage on several occasions in the past. Since the tunnel had not been discovered in over a decade, it was a time-honored way in which to quietly cross between Czechoslovakia and West Germany. The shaft was an ideal way for Phoenix Force to enter the country without dealing with red tape or possible security leaks.

At last the men reached the end of the tunnel. The mouth of the shaft was plugged by a boulder that was held in place by a number of steel bolts. Cernak unfastened the bolts and placed a brawny shoulder to the stone. Hahn assisted him, and together they pushed the boulder aside. The delightful scent of fresh air, tinted with the scent of evergreens, poured through the gap. All six men were greatly relieved to be able to breathe air that was not musty and stale.

They emerged from the tunnel to find themselves in the center of the famed Bohemian Forest. Tall pines surrounded the commandos. Branches formed a dark ceiling, all but blotting out the night sky above. None of the men used flashlights. The area was not ordinarily patrolled by Czech border personnel, although occasional security checks within the forest were not unheard of.

Yakov Katzenelenbogen shifted the strap of his canvas knapsack across his left shoulder. The bag contained his Uzi submachine gun, three hundred rounds of 9 mm slugs, grenades, some clothing and his trihook prosthesis. The Israeli favored this device because the three metal talons were more versatile than the stiff, five-fingered prosthesis. However, the latter device appeared more lifelike from a distance.

Manning, McCarter and Hahn did not have to worry about disguising missing limbs. Calvin James, however, had a more difficult problem to deal with. A black man in the Bohemian countryside could hardly pass as a native Czechoslovakian. His disguise was certainly not going to be inconspicuous, but it was the best they could do on such short notice.

James selected two long strips of bandages and began wrapping them around the back of his head, lower face and forehead. With some greasepaint—Caucasian flesh tone—he colored his exposed cheeks, ears and the bridge of his nose. A pair of dark glasses and a wide-brim hat completed the disguise.

"I feel like Claude Rains," James muttered, his voice muffled by the bandage.

"Just remember you're the victim of a terrible accident," Katz said. "You've been badly burned in a fire. You can't speak. You can hardly hear. And you're virtually blind."

"Your hands were also burned," Manning added. "I'll bandage them for you. Remember, you can't use your fingers very well."

"Does my dick work?" James asked dryly.

"Yes," McCarter assured him. "But if you take it out in public we'll have to bandage it, too."

"You'd like that, wouldn't you, sweetie?" James replied, his lips producing a kissing sound against the bandage that covered his mouth.

"Will you two lovebirds try to be serious?" Manning asked with mock gruffness. "We're on a deadly mission, you know."

"We'd better start walking if we want to reach Pizen by daybreak," Karl Hahn suggested, glancing at the luminous dial of his wristwatch.

"If we are stopped by any soldiers, let me talk with them before you pull out guns and start shooting," Cernak urged, well aware of what his companions carried in their knapsacks. He also knew that all five had pistols hidden under their jackets.

"We don't want to kill anyone unless there's no other way to handle the situation," Katz assured him.

"That is why you carry guns?" Cernak snorted. "I've never carried a weapon. If the Communists stop you and find guns, you are in big trouble."

"We'll be in bigger trouble if we don't have these guns and the Communists try to capture us," Katz insisted. "Don't worry about it, Alexei. We're not trigger-happy mad dogs. The guns are necessary. I thought Karl explained that."

"He tried," Cernak answered. "Well, I agreed to bring you here, so I'll keep my mouth shut about guns. But I'd rather you didn't shoot anybody when I'm around. I won't be able to help any more Czechs across the border if you get me killed."

"We have no intention of hurting your business that way," Gary Manning promised.

"Okay," Cernak replied. "I'm getting paid to help you. I like money the same as anybody else, but I'm also doing this because you say both Czechoslovakia and Germany will suffer if we don't stop the terrorists. I'm not so sure that people who kill Russians should be punished, but I don't want them making things harder for the country I was born in, or for the country I now am citizen of."

"We understand your reasons, Alexei," Katz stated.

"I hope you understand that most Czech soldiers are not terrorists or Communists," Cernak told him. "It's okay with me if you want to kill terrorists. Shit, I'll help you kill Communists. But if you have to kill Czechs, don't do it around me."

"Unless circumstances leave us no other choice," Hahn insisted. "You've got to be reasonable about this, Alexei."

"Reasonable?" The big Czech laughed. "If I were reasonable I doubt I would be here with you now, eh?"

"I think this bloke's a bit daft," McCarter whispered to Calvin James.

"Yeah," the black commando said softly through his bandage disguise. "There's a lot of that going around these days."

11

Alexei Cernak and the men of Phoenix Force walked along the side of a dirt road, heading northeast toward Pizen. They wore old clothing, smeared with dirt and plastered to their skin with sweat. The clothes were the same garments they had worn while traveling through the tunnel. They carried knapsacks over their shoulders, except for Calvin James, who was supposedly injured. He hobbled alongside Gary Manning on a pair of crudely made crutches. The powerful Canadian carried James's pack as well as his own. The extra burden did not bother Manning, because his strength and endurance doubled that of most men.

"Nice area," Manning mused, happily drawing the night air into his lungs as he glanced about at the forest. "Reminds me a little of Canada."

"I can't smell much," James commented. His nostrils were covered by the bandage. "Can't see much, either. Man, I'll be glad when I can take this shit off. This disguise is a real pain in the ass."

"Maybe we can arrange for our next mission to be in a nice integrated country," Manning said.

"Or some place like Haiti or Kenya," James commented. "Then maybe you guys will all have to make like Al Jolson and—"

The sound of motors interrupted his remark. Headlights appeared in the distance. Two vehicles were heading their way. As they approached, Phoenix Force recognized that the vehicles were military transport trucks. The first was actually an armored car complete with a mounted machine gun and a soldier posted at the trigger. The second truck was large enough to contain two dozen troopers.

"Shit," James rasped, wondering if he could still draw his Colt Commander from shoulder leather with a bandaged hand.

"Relax," Manning urged. "We're not in trouble yet."

The vehicles began to slow down as they drew closer. The beams of the headlights illuminated the six men and both vehicles came to a halt. Three soldiers hopped down from the back of the truck. Each carried a Model 58 assault rifle, the Czech version of the Russian Kalashnikov. An officer stepped from the armored car. The straps of his backpack concealed the rank on his shoulder boards, but his commanding manner left no doubt that he held a position of authority.

"Dobry vecer," Cernak said in a steady voice. "Good evening. Is there some problem, Captain?"

"It is *Lieutenant*," the officer stated as he stepped closer. "And I shall ask the questions. What are you men doing here at this late hour?"

"We are workers from the Otava Metal Parts Factory," Cernak answered. "They are trying to meet a deadline for machinery parts essential to a government project. No one tells us details, but they put us on the late shift. The factory is open twenty-four hours a day trying to meet that deadline...."

"So you just left work?" the lieutenant inquired. "We can check that story, my friend."

"We left the factory about a quarter after midnight," Karl Hahn announced, his Czech containing the proper central Bohemian accent. "Please check with Supervisor Husnik."

"I see." The lieutenant stared at their knapsacks, his youthful eyes narrowing slightly. "What are you carrying?"

"Tools, food, some clothes and medical supplies," Cernak answered. "My cousin was injured in an accident at work. My uncle is not well and is already a bit senile. His heart is not good and he is very clumsy at times."

The lieutenant gazed into Katz's face. The Israeli grinned at him, bobbing his head as he repeated, *"Dobry den! Dobry den!"*

"Hello, old man," the officer replied with a sympathetic nod. He turned his attention to the bandaged figure of Calvin James. "What happened to your cousin?"

"It was terrible, Lieutenant," Cernak replied. "Molten metal splashed over him. Burned him very badly. It burned his eyes, mouth, nose and hands."

"Are you certain he was not burned in a forest fire?" the officer demanded, his voice adopting a hard edge. "A fire that occurred at the border only fifty kilometers away. A fire that occurred less than four hours ago."

"Burns received that recently would still be raw and blistered," Hahn declared, his computerlike mind working at rapid speed. "Leos was injured six days ago. Scar tissue has already begun to form and his skin has a fused quality, with only a few open blisters. Would you care to see for yourself? If you have a strong stomach, that is?"

The lieutenant stared at James, considering what action to take. He shook his head and turned to Cernak and Hahn.

"This man has obviously suffered a great deal, and I have no desire to manhandle a blind cripple and cause him further distress," the officer announced.

"Mockrat dekuji," Cernak replied. "Thank you very much, Lieutenant. You are a good man."

"But I question what sort of men you are," the officer said sharply. "Your cousin should be in a hospital, or home in bed, recovering from his injury. And your uncle should not be out at this hour, either. Certainly neither can work at the factory."

"Do not underestimate my uncle, Lieutenant," Cernak said quickly. "He still likes to work and he won't stay home. It is easier for me to watch him at work. As long as we keep him away from the heavy machinery he is fine. My mother is not capable of taking care of either my uncle or poor Leos."

"Doesn't Leos have a wife?" the lieutenant asked.

"She left him after the accident," Cernak said sadly. "Just abandoned him like a broken doll."

"Heartless bitch," the lieutenant muttered. "But the state hospital should be looking after this man. Why isn't he being treated by proper medical personnel?"

"You'll have to ask Dr. Novtony," Hahn declared. "He released Leos. Said the sooner he started to adjust to the outside world the better. We're supposed to take him back for more treatment on Saturday."

"His treatment seems to be somewhat lacking," the officer said with a sigh. "Couldn't you at least manage some means of transportation?"

"Supervisor Husnik promised us he would give us a ride to and from work," Hahn answered. "But he was already gone when we finished our shift."

"Husnik," the lieutenant said, his tone dripping venom. "Do you know his first name?"

"I believe it is Alexei," Cernak replied quickly. "But he always refers to himself as 'Supervisor Husnik.'"

"Fascist pig," the officer muttered. "I shall have this man's conduct reported. I only wish I could give you a ride in our truck to your home, but I am under orders. You understand?"

"Rozumim," Cernak assured him. "Thank you for your consideration, Lieutenant."

"Take care of Leos and the old man," the officer instructed. "And watch out for strangers. There are some very dangerous men at large. They are cold-blooded killers and would show you no mercy if you got in their way."

"Does this concern the forest fire you spoke of?" Hahn inquired.

"I'm not at liberty to say," the lieutenant replied sadly. "But the men are dangerous and well armed. They were traveling in trucks, but may be on foot by now. Be very careful."

"We will, Lieutenant," Cernak promised. "Thank you."

"Rado se stalo," the young officer replied with a shrug.

The lieutenant and his soldiers climbed back into the vehicles. Cernak and the men of Phoenix Force waved at the troopers as they drove up the road. Several soldiers in the rear of the truck waved back and yelled, *"Sbohem!"* or goodbye.

"Jesus," Calvin James said with a deep sigh of relief. "I think my heart is still stuck in my throat."

"I know what you mean," Gary Manning replied with an earnest nod. "That was a little closer than I like."

"I tried to keep up with the conversation," Katz stated. "But my Czech isn't very good. You certainly handled yourself well, Karl. I didn't realize you spoke Czech so fluently."

"Neither did I," the German agent admitted. "Remarkable what you can do when you're terrified. We were lucky that the officer was young and softhearted. Otherwise we would have had some fireworks."

"Speaking of fire," Cernak began. "I wonder what that business about the forest fire was all about."

"Forest fire?" McCarter inquired. "Bear in mind, mates, not all of us understand the language."

"A forest fire is when a bunch of trees and bushes burn," Hahn said with a grin.

"Oh, thanks," the Briton snorted. "You're so much help."

"Seriously," Hahn added. "I think we found out just where Briggs and his boys got to. Unless there's a hell of a coincidence, they crashed through the border about four hours before we did. They're here in Czechoslovakia."

"Holy shit," James rasped. "Those dudes gotta be crazy to bust into the country like a bull in a china shop. Everybody from the neighborhood police to the KGB will be looking for them."

"And they'll be checking out strangers with extra care," Yakov Katzenelenbogen added. "Which isn't going to make our mission any easier."

"Nothing like a little extra challenge to liven things up a bit," McCarter said with a shrug.

CZECHOSLOVAKIA IS ROUGHLY DIVIDED into three sections: Slovakia, Moravia and Bohemia. The greatest population—and the seat of national power—is found in Bohemia. Czechoslovakia is the most industrialized of any East European nation and the only iron-curtain country to be a major steel producer and automobile manufacturer. It also has the highest standard of living of any Communist society with the exception of Hungary, which has managed to get away with "creeping capitalism" without inciting further Soviet military intervention.

Faroslav Zatopek owned an auto-repair shop in Pizen, one of the largest cities in western Bohemia. Because a fair number of Czechs own cars, Zatopek made a decent living. Naturally the state appropriated most of his income and paid him according to government policy. Yet Zatopek was financially comfortable by Czech standards. He had a wife, three children and he actively supported Communism.

However, there was another side to Faroslav Zatopek. Despite his public image, Zatopek hated Communism in general and the Soviet brand in particular. He was selective about whom he trusted. Zatopek was especially leery of agents from the West. The BND was riddled with moles and the American CIA was subject to security leaks that resulted in its secrets winding up on the front page of every major newspaper in the world.

Zatopek preferred to deal with individuals rather than organizations. A large number of "cutouts," or free-lance agents, operated in Europe. They are not directly connected to any government, although most are motivated by principles as opposed to profit. Most professional mercenaries are not simply "guns for hire" going to the highest bidder. A similar philosophy is followed among cutouts.

Alexei Cernak had worked with Zatopek many times in the past. Zatopek was also familiar with Karl Hahn, although he did not realize that Hahn was a member of the BND. Hahn understood the Czech's apprehension with regard to government agencies and sympathized with Zatopek's sensitive position. Hahn's well-deserved reputation as a maverick was due to his knowledge of the world of espionage. He kept secrets from his superiors because his superiors could not be trusted to maintain security. Hahn had let Zatopek believe he was a free-lance agent. Considering the German's method of operating in the field, this was really just a distortion of the truth.

Zatopek had never turned away a friend in need. When Hahn and Cernak arrived at his door with four strangers, Zatopek did not ask any questions until they could talk safely. He led the visitors through a trapdoor in the floor of his office to a room hidden beneath his auto-repair shop.

"This is probably the most secure safe house in Czechoslovakia," Cernak assured the men of Phoenix Force. "No need to worry about hidden microphones or peepholes here."

"One can never be too careful," Katz replied. He turned to Zatpoek and added, "I don't doubt your security, but one should never become too confident in this business."

"I agree, my friend," Zatopek assured him, speaking fluent German with a proper Bavarian accent. The Czech possessed a working knowledge of five languages, including English, but he had truly mastered only two. "Carelessness can be a fatal ailment."

Zatopek was a few years younger than Katz, although he appeared to be much older. He was fat; rolls of lard hung over his belt and hung loosely from his chin. Only a fringe of gray hair remained on his round dome. Zatopek often smiled, although his eyes contained a trace of sadness. The Czech had seen much sorrow living in a country that had suffered greatly under the tyranny of both the Nazi occupation and Communist control.

"This looks like a good safe house," Gary Manning began, glancing about the basement. The stone walls appeared sturdy and the ceiling was thick. "The only thing that bothers me is the fact that there's only one way into or out of this room. If the STB or KGB find us, we'd be boxed in here. There's no way to escape and little chance to hold them back."

"Yeah," James added. "One lousy grenade could wipe us all out with one big bang."

"The Communists haven't discovered my safe house in almost twenty years," Zatopek assured him. "They won't find it now unless one of you makes a mistake and leads them here."

"We try to keep mistakes at a minimum," Katz stated. He wished he could light a cigarette, but the basement was poorly ventilated. "Alexei tells us you've got connections within the party and the Czech military."

"That is correct," Zatopek said proudly. "They think I am a dedicated Communist, so they trust me. I'm sort of the guardian for this neighborhood. I spread their propaganda, making certain I'm very pompous and obnoxious in the process. Only those already brainwashed by the Soviets are impressed. I certainly won't convert any non-Communists. Most of them hate my guts."

"You'd better be careful," Katz warned. "You might get a knife in the ribs from a supporter of the actual cause you're fighting for. Irony isn't amusing when it costs someone's life."

"Irony," Zatopek said with a laugh. "It is rather ironic that I am helping you stop so-called terrorists who are killing Russians."

"Don't misunderstand our reason for being here," Manning told him. "And don't sympathize with the terrorists. These people aren't going to help Czechoslovakia throw out the Soviets. They're more apt to encourage the Russians to increase their troop strength in your country and enforce even greater controls. So far, all they've accomplished by knocking off a few Soviet personnel has been to anger the KGB. The Russians have killed a number of American and West German agents in retaliation."

"Certainly isn't going to improve anything." Zatopek sighed. "The sad thing is, the terrorists probably think they're doing the right thing."

"Most people think they're always doing the right thing," Karl Hahn remarked. "One can justify any sort of behavior. Even blowing up a roomful of innocent people."

"Are you chaps discussing anything we should know about, too?" David McCarter asked, a trace of annoyance in his tone. The Briton and Calvin James could not understand the conversation since the others were speaking German.

"Don't worry," Manning replied. "We'll give you the translated version later."

"I'll check with my sources," Zatopek promised. "But I hope you understand that I don't have any direct connections to the STB or KGB. Most of what I hear are simply rumors."

"Just do the best you can," Katz urged. "And thank you for your help."

"You gentlemen better get some sleep," Zatopek suggested. "Tomorrow will probably be a busy day for us all."

12

"I hope you gentlemen followed my advice," Faroslav Zatopek announced as he descended the ladder to the safe house. "I think I have some important information."

The Czech nearly lost his grip on the ladder rungs when he noticed that all five men of Phoenix Force held weapons. Katz, Manning and Hahn had lowered their firearms when they recognized Zatopek's voice. McCarter and James, because they did not understand German, did not realize that it was Zatopek until he had come close enough to be recognized in the dim light of the basement hideout.

"Sorry, man," Calvin James muttered as he laid his .45 caliber Colt Commander on his cot.

"Don't worry, Herr Zatopek," Karl Hahn assured their host. "Just a reflex reaction. Tell us your news."

"News?" Zatopek was disoriented. He was not accustomed to having guns pointed at him. "Of course. I just returned from a tavern at Kladno. It is a favorite spot for off-duty soldiers. Naturally there are always spies planted among the crowd—STB, KGB and probably an occasional agent working for the West. A couple of soldiers were discussing their recent guard duty at the Jaroslav Heyrovsky Clinic."

"The clinic is located near Karlovy Vary," Alexei Cernak informed the others. "The city is better known to Westerners as Carlsbad. It is a very historic city, although the Heyrovsky Clinic was built less than a year ago."

"Correct," Zatopek said with a short nod. His curt gesture suggested that he found Cernak's interruption annoying. "The soldiers said that all the patients who were originally at the clinic had to be moved to other hospitals. Several bodies were carried into the clinic on stretchers by men who wore heavy protective suits complete with hoods and masks. The soldiers were afraid to stand guard at the place. They thought the dead men had been victims of a biological-warfare virus."

"Jesus," Manning rasped. "Do you think that Briggs would actually be crazy enough to haul some sort of CBW virus across the border?"

"Briggs might be capable of it," Katz answered. "But he crashed through the fence only a few hours before we did. If the soldiers Herr Zatopek met at the tavern had really been guarding a quarantined area, they wouldn't be allowed to leave the spot for at least twenty-four hours."

"The soldiers said that they had been stationed at the Heyrovsky Clinic earlier this week," Zatopek said with a sigh. "I guess it isn't connected, after all."

"Not necessarily," Hahn stated. "The terrorism in Czechoslovakia started long before Briggs crashed the fence. If Briggs is behind the previous acts it means he already had some of his people operating within the country. Maybe there is a connection and maybe there isn't."

"Unfortunately the soldiers apparently knew very little and seemed to be guessing about the dead men," Zatopek continued. "They suspected that the bodies had been flown to the clinic from the site of a recent train derailment that happened near the White Carpathians, part of the mountain range that separates Moravia and Slovakia. There are rumors of a chemical spill in the area."

"Could be a coincidence," Katz mused. "What else did they say?"

"One of them told a comrade that they were required to wear protective clothing inside the building for the first twenty-four hours," Zatopek answered. "After that, Professor Casavska decided that the special gear wasn't necessary."

"Wait a minute," Hahn said sternly. "Casavska was examining the bodies? Would that be Professor Emil Casavska?"

"Wasn't he that scientist who was thrown in jail for organizing a rally in support of a nuclear-weapons freeze?" Gary Manning inquired.

"That's right," the BND agent confirmed. "Antinuke demonstrations are common in the United States, Great Britain and in other democracies. In West Germany, the Green Party constantly organizes marches and demonstrations. But unless the demonstrators trespass on private property, cause some sort of vandalism, or become a public nuisance, none of them gets arrested. And even if they are, they usually just get a fine. The same sort of protest in a Communist country would result in at least six months in a mental rehabilitation hospital or even a political prison."

"Bet that wouldn't happen if the protests were directed against the nuclear weapons belonging to Western democracies and NATO," Manning snorted. "Have you ever noticed that the loudest advocates of a nuclear ban seldom mention the weapons owned by the Soviet Union or the Warsaw Pact countries?"

"Well, Professor Casavska did," Hahn said with a shrug. "He called on the Czechoslovakian government and the Soviet Union to put a freeze on nuclear weapons as a goodwill gesture toward the West in order to encourage total disarmament in the future. It was embarrassing for the state because Casavska is one of the best known nuclear physicists in Czechoslovakia. They decided the professor must have suffered a nervous breakdown, and sent him to a reeducation center to help him get a 'grip on reality.' Something like that.''

"The state wouldn't have agreed to release Casavska and send him to the Heyrovsky Clinic unless it was a serious matter,'' Yakov Katzenelenbogen stated. "Do you know if Casavska is still there?''

"The soldiers didn't say,'' Zatopek replied. "Two men in plainclothes said something to them. Probably STB, warning them to shut up. The soldiers were followed by one of the agents when they left the tavern. They were lucky. The KGB would probably have had them arrested on the spot.''

"Is there any way you can find out if the professor is still there without attracting suspicion?'' Katz asked.

"I think so,'' Zatopek said with a nod.

"I'll check with my connections, too,'' Cernak added. "Between the two of us we should be able to find out everything you want to know about the clinic and who's there.''

"We'll need any details you can get,'' Katz urged. "Try to find out if there are any patients or regular staff at the clinic and the number of security guards posted. Also, any information about surveillance cameras and alarms or other security devices would be most helpful. But most important, find out if the personnel inside the clinic are wearing protective gear.''

"You plan to break into the Jaroslav Heyrovsky Clinic?'' Zatopek glared at the Phoenix Force commander. "That's insane!''

"It's also the only possible lead we've got,'' Katz replied simply. "Maybe the clinic won't answer any questions for us, but we've got to find out.''

"What if I refuse to help you?'' Zatopek demanded.

"We can't force you to do anything you feel is too risky, Faroslav,'' Karl Hahn told him. "But remember what's at stake. I've known you for some time, and I know how much you love your country. You're familiar with the history of Czechoslovakia. I don't have to remind you that every time there's been a major conflict in Europe, Czechoslovakia has been in the middle of it."

"Unfortunate geography." Cernak sighed. "We're dead center."

"Exactly," Hahn agreed. "If the acts of terrorism against Soviet personnel continue, and if the cold war heats up, Czechoslovakia will become everybody's battleground. If a major war between the superpowers of the East and West occurs, Czechoslovakia will be torn to pieces."

"I didn't say I *wouldn't* help," Zatopek said with a shrug. "How soon will you need this information?"

"As soon as possible," Katz replied.

KARLOVY VARY, or Carlsbad, is one of the most popular cities in Czechoslovakia. From a distance it appears to be the perfect postcard image of the popular concept of Eastern Europe. The Gothic architectural style is evident throughout the city. The streets form complete rings within Carlsbad, a circular design that was popular during the Holy Roman Empire in the ninth century.

The city is famous for its mineral-water spas. Peter the Great, Beethoven and Goethe were among the believers in the reputed healing qualities of the waters. Carlsbad is also known as the home of the world-renown Moser crystal.

The Jaroslav Heyrovsky Clinic was located roughly three kilometers south of Karlovy Vary. Named in honor of the winner of the 1959 Nobel Prize for chemistry, the clinic was a small medical center that specialized in treating victims of genetic diseases. Under ordinary conditions, armed soldiers did not stand guard at the Heyrovsky Clinic. The place had no military significance and it was located in northern Bohemia, near the East German border.

Zatopek's sources had learned that security at the Heyrovsky Clinic was not exceptionally tight. An iron picket fence, designed to keep noisy children away from the grounds, surrounded the building. It would not deter serious invaders. However, the soldiers stationed at the clinic patroled the area and two sentries were posted at the front gate.

Apparently there were no surveillance cameras or heat sensors installed at the clinic. None of the original patients or hospital staff had returned to the building, although the personnel were no longer required to wear protective gear. Professor Casavska was still inside the clinic and the mysterious corpses had not been removed. Zatopek was unable to learn any other details about the dead men or Casavska's investigation.

Phoenix Force decided to make their move at dusk because sentries tend to be less alert at early twilight and daybreak. One assumes that trouble will either arrive during night or day, as if the minutes between these conditions are some sort of safety zone. A somewhat disgruntled Alexei Cernak had agreed to transport Phoenix Force to the site. He drove a truck around the area, allowing the commandos to observe the clinic via field glasses.

"Shit," Calvin James remarked as he lowered his binoculars. "That setup is a piece of cake."

"They're never as easy as they look," Gary Manning stated, inserting a tranquilizer dart into the breech of an Anschutz air rifle.

Cernak glanced over his shoulder at the five men in the back of the truck. They were busily preparing their weapons. Every member of Phoenix Force carried a pistol in a special shoulder-holster rig designed to accommodate the bulk of an attached silencer. Yet they left their full-auto weapons in knapsacks. The raid on the clinic required cleverness and good timing more than it required firepower.

"You told me you wouldn't kill any Czech soldiers unless you had to," Cernak reminded them as he steered the truck onto Masaryk Avenue.

"With a little luck we'll be able to get into the clinic without having to kill anyone," Katz assured him. The Israeli looked terribly vulnerable. He was dressed in a dirt-stained gray suit. Katz did not wear a prosthesis. The empty sleeve of his jacket hung from the stump of his right arm. The cloth of the sleeve had been shredded and laced with red ink.

"Pull over to the curb and let us out, Alexei," Karl Hahn instructed as he slid a hard, black rubber tube into his belt at the small of his back. The German covered the truncheon by pulling on his jacket.

"All right," Cernak replied, checking the mirror in case a police car had taken an interest in the truck.

"Remember to give us about an hour," Katz reminded Cernak.

"I'll drive around Carlsbad for a while," the Czech replied. "I'm worried that you're all going to get killed and that I'm going to wind up in the hands of the fucking KGB."

"Just don't run out on us, mate," David McCarter warned as he switched on the safety to a Bio-Inoculator dart pistol.

"Take it easy, man," James told the Briton, tucking his own B-I pistol into his belt. "Alexei isn't a coward. He wouldn't be here if he was."

"You're right," McCarter agreed. "Sorry, Alexei. Guess I'm a bit nervous myself."

"Yeah," Manning muttered. "We need to turn you loose on somebody to work off some of that frustration."

"I'm glad you understand," McCarter said with a wolfish grin.

The five members of Phoenix Force pushed through the canvas flap at the rear of the truck and jumped to the ground. They hastily approached the Heyrovsky Clinic, moving toward a column of trees along the outside of the fence. Manning, James and McCarter used the trees for cover while Hahn and Katz headed for the front gate. The Israeli leaned against Hahn and hung his head low, moaning as he clutched at his "bloodied" stump with his left hand. Katz and Hahn were gifted actors. The German appeared distressed as he helped the "wounded" Katzenelenbogen to the gate.

"Pomoc! Prosim, pomoc!" Hahn cried as he half dragged Katz to the gate.

The sentries responded to his cry for help by unslinging Model 58 rifles from their shoulders. However, the soldiers pointed the barrels of the guns toward the sky when they saw Katz and Hahn. Since the elder man's right arm was obviously severed at the elbow and the torn sleeve appeared to be stained with fresh blood, the guards did not regard them as a potential threat.

"Pomoc," Hahn rasped. *"Nalehavy pripad..."*

"We can see you have an emergency," one of the sentries replied gruffly. "What happened?"

"An accident," Hahn explained. "My friend's arm was caught in a machine. The gears tore it right off at the elbow. He must get medical help immediately."

"There's a hospital in Karlovy Vary," a sentry replied. "You'll have to take him there."

"He'll bleed to death by then," Hahn snapped, glaring through the bars at the sentries. "I don't have a car. Do you think I can carry him into the city and find the hospital in time?"

"I'll get Captain Kostey," one of the guards declared. "If he'll allow us to use a jeep, we'll drive you into the city. All right?"

"Ano," Hahn replied gratefully. *"Je to od vas velmi mile."*

"We're not kind," the senior soldier replied. "We're just servants of the people's army and therefore concerned with the welfare of all Czech citizens."

Both soldiers slung their rifles on their shoulders once more. The sergeant picked up the receiver from a field telephone and dialed two numbers. He spoke into the phone, nodding as he listened to a reply.

"Open the gate," he told the other sentry. "The captain will be here with a medic to treat this poor man. He's also getting a driver to transport these gentlemen to the hospital."

"Mockrat dekuji," Hahn thanked the sergeant.

The guards opened the gate as an officer and another enlisted man approached from the clinic. Hahn assisted Katz across the threshold. Captain Kostey, a tall officer with deep lines etched into his lean face, wearily nodded at the two civilians. He gestured for the medic to approach.

Katz groaned and staggered forward, nearly colliding with the medic. The soldier tried to catch Katz before the older man harmed himself. The Phoenix Force commander suddenly pivoted, smashing the stump of his right arm into the side of the medic's jaw. The skin and muscle of Katz's arm had healed long ago. The veteran warrior could deliver a devastating, if unorthodox, punch with the stump. The medic's head spun from the blow and he wilted to the ground.

"Co... ?" the startled officer began.

Captain Kostey was not sure if Katz had attacked the soldier or he had simply gone berserk with pain. He was not sure how to handle the one-armed man. Katz solved the problem for Kostey. He had drawn a Nova XR5000 from his left-hand jacket pocket. Katz suddenly lunged in a fencer's thrust, jamming the metal prods of the stun gun under the captain's rib cage.

Katz pressed the button of the compact Nova. Thirty-five thousand volts shot through Captain Kostey's body. The charge was a powerful jolt, although the Nova XR5000 produces electricity with less than one amp. The charge has a dramatic effect on human flesh without being fatal. Kostey's body stiffened as the volts branched through his nervous system.

The two sentries had turned their attention toward the unexpected conflict between Katz and their fellow soldiers. Karl Hahn instantly took advantage of the diversion. He swiftly drew the rubber truncheon from the small of his back and clubbed the sergeant behind the ear. The rubber club had long been used by the West German police for taking out an opponent without causing physical injury. The cudgel rendered the NCO unconscious in a single blow.

As the sergeant began to fall, the other sentry turned to see Hahn swing the black rubber weapon once more. The truncheon caught the soldier on the point of his chin. He fell to one knee, dazed but still conscious. The trooper raised an arm to shield his head from more blows. Hahn snapped his wrist, whipping the club across the man's forearm. Hahn immediately delivered another strike to the side of his opponent's neck. The soldier groaned as he slumped to the ground.

"Thanks for your cooperation," Katz told Captain Kostey as he stepped over the officer's inert form.

A guard patroling the grounds near the fence witnessed the confrontation. The fight had occurred so swiftly that the soldier was not certain of what had happened until he saw four of his comrades sprawled on the ground and two strangers heading toward the clinic. The soldier unslung his rifle, but held his fire. He decided that his first priority was to alert the others to danger. The guard unhooked a two-way radio from his belt and raised it to his mouth.

A sharp needle of pain pierced his nape. He yelped and swatted a hand to his neck. His fingers plucked a feathered object from his skin. The trooper stared at the tranquilizer dart with amazement. Two hundred milligrams of Thorazine rapidly traveled through his blood to his brain. The guard dropped his radio and passed out.

David McCarter jumped down from a tree limb that extended over the top of the fence. The Briton held his Bio-Inoculator ready as he stepped toward the unconscious soldier. The B-I pistol is electrically operated by a built-in battery and resembles a Government Issue Colt with a plug over the hammer section and a cord attached to the butt.

"Co je toto?" a voice inquired behind McCarter.

The Briton whirled, aiming his Bio-Inoculator at the sound of the speaker's voice. A startled Czech trooper stared back at him, his rifle slung over his shoulder. McCarter triggered the B-I gun. A dart struck the soldier in the chest, but he was able to bring his rifle around and aim it at the Briton.

"Shit," McCarter muttered as he squeezed the trigger again.

The Bio-Inoculator did not fire.

McCarter had only one chance. He threw himself to the ground and tumbled into a fast shoulder roll. His hand streaked inside the jacket for the Browning Hi-Power. McCarter did not think about the likelihood of drawing his pistol before his opponent could aim and fire. The British warrior did not have time to think. He merely reacted, swiftly and efficiently, in the only manner circumstances allowed.

The Browning cleared leather as he pivoted on one knee and swung the silenced pistol in the direction of the Czech soldier. He snapped off the safety catch and began to squeeze the trigger. McCarter's finger tensed as he forced himself not to complete the movement that was so natural to him.

The soldier had fallen to the ground; the rifle was now lying beside his quiet body. McCarter sighed in relief as he returned the Browning to shoulder leather.

"Must've just taken a while for the drug to take effect," he thought aloud.

McCarter retrieved his Bio-Inoculator and examined the weapon. The cord connecting the firing mechanism with the battery had popped loose at the butt. The Briton clucked his tongue with disgust. Fancy newfangled gizmos are as apt to break down as to bloody well work, he thought. Yet he realized the B-I pistol was a good nonlethal weapon that he had used several times in the past without a misfire. Any weapon can malfunction and the Bio-Inoculator was not a particularly new invention. It had been used by the CIA for more than ten years. The Church Committee investigation of alleged Company misconduct in the mid-seventies had been horrified to learn about this insidious device. However, Senator Church and his committee did not express similar alarm about the KGB cyanide-gas pen or the umbrella germ inoculator used to assassinate Bulgarian defector George Markov in 1978.

CALVIN JAMES HAD TAKEN OUT another guard at the east side of the fence. The black commando checked the Czech trooper's eyes to be certain that the man was unconscious. He gathered up the soldier's Model 58 and carried the rifle to a side door of the clinic. James removed the magazine from the M-58 and worked the bolt to double-check that the weapon was empty. He tossed the rifle behind some bushes and knelt by the door.

"I sure wish Rafael was here," James muttered as he removed a small leather packet from inside his jacket. Encizo was the force's break-and-enter expert. This time James would have to manage on his own.

He placed his Bio-Inoculator on the ground within easy reach and then unzipped the packet. It contained a number of lock picks. James selected two instruments and started to work the lock.

Suddenly the door burst open. It slammed into James, knocking him onto his back. A Czech soldier charged across the threshold and nearly tripped over the black warrior. The trooper gasped in surprise when he saw James on the ground. He pointed a compact Skorpion machine pistol at the black man and prepared to squeeze the trigger.

James braced himself as he prepared to launch a roundhouse kick from the prone position. His boot struck the soldier's Skorpion, kicking the subgun from the Czech's grasp. James shifted his weight to one side in order to thrust another kick into the startled man's abdomen. The edge of his foot rammed into the soldier's gut just above the groin.

The trooper doubled up in pain. James quickly slashed a kick across the soldier's face. The back of his heel caught the guy hard on the jawbone. The Czech fell against the doorway and slid senseless to the floor. James rose to his feet and reached for the Bio-Inoculator.

The metallic slide and snap of a rifle bolt drew his attention to the doorway. Another soldier stood at the threshold, fumbling with an assault rifle. James did not have time to pick up the B-I pistol, aim and fire it. He jumped forward and extended a leg as he sailed through the doorway.

The black commando's boot crashed into the Czech's M-58. The kick drove the frame of the rifle into the soldier's chest. The blow drove him backward into a wall. James landed nimbly on his feet and lashed a tae kwon-do snap kick to the trooper's groin. The man uttered a choking gasp and folded at the middle. James chopped the side of his left hand into the nerve center just behind the man's collarbone and followed with another karate stroke to the base of his opponent's neck. The Czech dropped his rifle and fell on his face. He had been knocked unconscious.

A sudden movement caused James to whirl. Yet another Czech soldier charged toward James, swinging the butt of his Model 58 at the black man's head. The Phoenix fighter dodged the attack. The walnut stock cracked against tile when it struck the wall instead of James's skull.

The Phoenix pro's left hand grabbed the rifle barrel to prevent the soldier from using the weapon as his right fist drove a hard uppercut to the man's solar plexus. The trooper groaned, but held on to his rifle. James pumped a knee between his opponent's legs. A high-pitched whine escaped from the man's throat. The black badass seized the back of the soldier's head and rammed the fellow's forehead into the wall. James knocked the Czech's head against a wall a second time to be sure he was unconscious before letting the man drop to the floor.

"This job doesn't pay enough," James rasped, trying to catch his breath.

He had been too busy just staying alive to examine his immediate surroundings. James found himself in a long corridor. The immaculate walls and floor were white tile. Mercury lights burned from the ceiling. A column of doors was located along one wall. The doors were numbered and labeled in Czechoslovakian, which did not help James determine what the rooms might be.

The soldiers he had encountered had obviously been expecting trouble. That meant time was running out fast. James did not bother trying to retrieve his Bio-Inoculator. He drew the silencer-equipped Colt Commander from shoulder leather. James moved to the closest door and turned the handle. It was not locked.

He stood clear of the doorway and used a short back kick to force the door open. No shots were fired in response.

James carefully entered the room with his pistol held ready. His precautions proved unnecessary because the room was unoccupied. Except for an empty bed and a small desk, the room was not even furnished. James turned and headed back to the hallway.

A bullet smashed into the door, narrowly missing the black man's right shoulder. He ducked into the room as the report of a pistol shot echoed through the corridor. James dropped to one knee and peered around the edge of the doorway, exposing only one eye and the muzzle of his silenced Colt.

A stocky figure dressed in a dark-gray suit stood at the threshold of a room labeled *Rentgenovy Snimek*. He held a CZ Model 75 pistol in his fist, a weapon that might be described as a cross between a Browning Hi-Power and a SIG-P220. The gunman did not notice James until it was too late. The black warrior canted the aim of his Colt Commander and squeezed the trigger.

The Czech screamed as a big .45 caliber bullet punched through his belly and tore apart his stomach. The guy fired his M-75 as he staggered backward, blood oozing from his wrecked abdomen. A 9 mm projectile bit into plaster above James's head as he triggered the Colt once more. The silenced Colt coughed harshly and a second .45 slug hit the Czech gunman in the center of the chest. The impact bowled the man over and dumped him on the floor in a dying heap.

James bolted across the hall to the *Rentenovy Snimek* room. A short, emaciated man stood near an X-ray machine with his hands raised to shoulder level. He wore a white hospital smock two sizes too large for his scrawny frame. His dark eyes registered surprise rather than fear. James smiled at the man and bowed slightly.

"Professor Cassivaska, I presume?" he inquired.

"Uh . . . Casavska," the scientist replied with a nod.

"I'll practice pronouncing your name later, man," James told him. "Let's go."

13

A Czech soldier emerged from the front entrance of the clinic with an M-58 rifle in his fists. He prepared to aim the weapon at the approaching figures of Yakov Katzenelen-bogen and Karl Hahn. He did not suspect that Gary Manning, stationed in the branches of a tree, watched him through the lenses of a Bushnell scope that was mounted on his Anschutz air rifle.

The cross hairs of the Bushnell found the side of the soldier's neck. Manning squeezed the trigger. A hypo dart rocketed into the man's flesh. The needle tip pierced the carotid artery, injecting a heavy dose of Thorazine. The guy opened his mouth in mute astonishment, dropped his rifle and stumbled forward. His dazed body tumbled down the front steps as Katz and Hahn charged up them.

The pair plunged into a small lobby. A Czech corporal was desperately working the frequency dial of a field radio as he sat behind the registration counter. All he had been able to find on the radio was crackling static. This was to be expected, since Manning had switched on a magnetic ionizer the moment he had seen Katz and Hahn overpower the four soldiers at the gate. The ionizer had been constructed by Karl Hahn. The device was simply a transmitter dish with a power pack that emitted a strong electromagnetic wave. This effectively scrambled any sort of radio transmission or reception within the clinic.

The corporal decided that the radio was useless. He swung around in his swivel chair and reached for an assault rifle. It was propped against the switchboard, which was the conventional means of communication within the clinic when it was not being occupied by Czech troops. Karl Hahn had drawn a Bio-Inoculator from his belt and quickly pumped a sleep dart into the soldier's back. The needle stabbed the fellow between the shoulder blades. He moaned as he slipped from the chair and fell to the floor.

A sergeant and a young lieutenant rushed through a corridor to the lobby. Both men were armed with pistols, but their weapons were still holstered. They were unaware that invaders had entered the clinic, although they had heard the pistol shot inside the building.

"Zameka, zavolejte bezpecnost!" the lieutenant ordered as he approached the front desk.

The pair came to an abrupt halt when they saw Katz and Hahn. The muzzle of the Israeli's silenced SIG-Sauer automatic pointed at the Czech soldiers. Both the officer and his sergeant raised their hands in surrender.

"Kdo jste?" the lieutenant demanded, trying to sound tough, but failing miserably. "Who are you?"

"To nevadi," Karl Hahn replied as he approached the pair. "It doesn't matter."

"Jak se mate?" Katz inquired, using one of the few expressions in Czechoslovakian that he could speak with a proper Bohemian accent. "How are you?"

The soldiers were startled by the question and stared at the Israeli. This distracted the pair long enough for Karl Hahn to slip behind them. The German quickly drew his *gummiknueppel* and struck the sergeant. The NCO crumbled to the floor. The lieutenant trembled as he saw the black rubber truncheon in Hahn's fist.

"Jak se jmenujete?" Hahn asked, lowering his club.

"My name?" the officer replied in surprise. "I am Lieutenant Pyotr Drevo. I will give you no more information than that."

"Kde je Casavska?" Katz demanded as he stepped closer, aiming the pistol at Drevo's face.

"I will not tell you . . ." the lieutenant began.

"You'll either tell us where to find Casavska or we'll kill you," Hahn warned. "If you don't tell us, we'll probably find him, anyway. That would make your death quite pointless, Lieutenant."

"He's X-raying one of the corpses in the east wing," the officer said quickly.

"Dekuji," Hahn thanked him, and then promptly clubbed Drevo behind the ear with his truncheon.

The lieutenant sighed as he slumped to a spot on the floor next to the sleeping sergeant. Hahn told Katz where the professor was located. The commandos headed for the east wing.

The hallway branched into an ell. Katz and Hahn approached the corner carefully. The German peered around the edge. He glimpsed two uniformed figures armed with Skorpion machine pistols heading toward their position. Hahn recoiled from the corner as a hail of 7.65 mm slugs blasted a fist-sized chunk of tile and plaster from the corner of the wall.

"Company," the BND man told Katz. He tossed the Bio-Inoculator into his left hand and drew the Walther P-5 autoloader from its shoulder holster with his right.

"They're armed with full-auto weapons," Katz added, glancing about for something that might help to even the odds.

Both men saw a large brass fire extinguisher at the same time. Katz, holding his pistol in combat readiness, stepped aside and let Hahn remove it from its mount on the wall. The Israeli realized there were certain things a two-handed man could do better than even the most able amputee. The Phoenix Force commander was too professional to allow pride to interfere with their chances for survival.

Hahn shoved the Walther and the B-I pistol into his belt and rapidly pulled the fire extinguisher from the wall. He tilted the contraption upside down and poked the nozzle around the corner. The German triggered the firing lever. Chemical foam jetted from the extinguisher, splashing the Czech troopers.

Muffled cries announced that the foam had splattered their eyes and their open mouths. One of the soldiers blindly fired a quick volley in desperation. Bullets burrowed into a wall more than six feet from Katz and Hahn. Satisfied that the gunmen were disabled and disoriented, the Phoenix pair stepped around the corner and opened fire.

The SIG-Sauer and Walther pistols spat fire through their sound suppressors. Parabellum rounds crashed into the Czech soldiers. The troopers fell to the tile floor, their uniforms stained with partially melted fire-extinguisher foam and fresh blood.

"Alexei will be pissed with us," Hahn said with a sigh.

"We promised Cernak we wouldn't kill anyone unless we had to," Katz told him with a shrug. "Well, we had to."

Two figures appeared at the opposite end of the hall. Katz and Hahn swung their weapons toward the shapes, but held their fire when they recognized Calvin James. The black warrior was escorting a thin, middle-aged man at gunpoint. James smiled at his teammates as he approached the pair.

"You guys have been busy," James remarked, noticing the slain soldiers on the floor.

"Yeah," Katz replied. "But I see you found the brass ring. I take it this is Professor Casavska."

"I sure hope so," James said. "Dude doesn't seem to speak English, but I've managed to make myself understood so far. Point a gun at somebody and they usually obey sign language just fine. By the way, I had to waste a dude who was with him. He was either STB or KGB or some other set of initials."

"*Dobry den, Pana Casavska,*" Hahn said to the professor. "*Pojd'te se mnou, prosim.*"

"Please come with you?" Casavska replied in Czech, his tone slightly amused. "Do I have a choice?"

"I'm afraid not," the German admitted. "And we don't have time to discuss this. Come on, Professor."

GARY MANNING JUMPED DOWN from the tree, swinging from a branch that extended over the fence. The Canadian unslung the Anschutz from his shoulder and headed for the rear of the clinic to cover the back of the building. He nearly ran head-on into four Czech soldiers armed with Model 58 rifles.

The Canadian lashed out with the barrel of his air rifle, deflecting the aim of the closest soldier's M-58. Barrel clanged against barrel. Manning's shoulders revolved sharply as he hooked the buttstock of his Anschutz into the trooper's face, breaking the soldier's jawbone with one hit.

Manning swung a cross-body slash with the Anschutz barrel. It struck the frame of another soldier's rifle, nearly knocking the weapon from the Czech's grasp. The Canadian's left fist hooked a short punch to the guy's temple and he followed with a kick to his opponent's gut. The second soldier fell to all fours as a third Czech stepped forward and swung a butt stroke at Manning's skull.

The Canadian ducked under the whistling walnut stock. The M-58 brushed the hairs on the top of his head, causing a cold jolt of fear to shoot through Manning's spinal cord, but not putting him out of action. The powerful Phoenix crusader rammed a short chop with the edge of the Anschutz stock under his attacker's ribs. The man gasped as the blow drove the breath from his lungs. Manning raised the Anschutz, using the frame as a solid bar. It struck the soldier's wrists and sent the M-58 hurtling from his grasp.

The fourth man, like his comrades, had hesitated to open fire with his rifle for fear of shooting one of his companions. However, he was not eager to lock horns with the fierce Canadian powerhouse. The soldier stepped away from the battle and raised his M-58 to his shoulder. He switched the selector to semiauto and aimed carefully, planning to put a bullet right between Manning's eyes.

The Canadian saw the fourth soldier out of the corner of his eye. He quickly whipped the Anschutz forward, holding it in one fist like an oversized pistol and snap-aiming. He triggered the air rifle before his opponent could open fire. The soldier's head jerked when the dart struck. He stared at Manning, his right eye wide open. The left eye vanished, replaced by the feathered end of a sleep dart. The needle tip had pierced the iris to the brain. The man died on his feet. He fell backward, the Model 58 still clenched in his fists.

The Czech that Manning had disarmed was not out of the fight yet. He took advantage of Manning's preoccupation with the fourth soldier. The Czech lunged for Manning's Anschutz. He grabbed the air rifle and twisted hard, wrenching it from the Canadian's hand. The soldier growled like an enraged beast and thrust the buttstock at Manning's face.

The Phoenix Force commando weaved his head from the path of the butt stroke. The rifle flashed past his left ear. A hard current of air brushed his face. Manning responded with a fast left jab to his opponent's sternum. The soldier grunted and stumbled slightly. Manning took a step forward and hooked his left fist into the Czech's kidney.

The Canadian warrior moved behind the trooper and hammered the bottom of his fist between the soldier's shoulder blades. The blow knocked the man to his knees. He braced his hands on the ground and started to rise. Manning raised his boot and stomped the heel into the base of the Czech's spine. The stomp snapped the coccyx. The soldier's mouth opened in mute agony. His eyes rolled up inside his head and he fainted.

Manning sighed with relief and stepped over his senseless opponent. He bent to gather up his Anschutz rifle. The Canadian stopped when the heard the snap of metal against metal. One of the Czech troops had switched the selector on his rifle. The soldier propped himself on one knee and aimed the M-58 at Manning. Blood drooled from a corner of his mouth as the Czech smiled. His finger began to squeeze the trigger.

The shot startled Manning. The Canadian winced. For a moment he thought he actually felt the hot projectile smash into his body, shearing through flesh and ripping his innards with swift violence. But this was only his imagination. Manning had not been hit.

The soldier had slumped to the ground. A bullet had burst a hole in the left side of his skull. A pool of crimson formed at the opposite side of his head where the exiting bullet had shattered a large portion of bone.

"You all right, mate?" a familiar voice called down from a second-story window.

Manning gazed up at David McCarter. The Briton held his Browning Hi-Power in a two-handed grip. He had removed the silencer after he heard two previous shots. The need for stealth had ended, and a silencer also reduces accuracy because it covers the front sight of the weapon.

"I'm okay, thanks," Manning called up to his partner. "What are you doing up there?"

"Figured I'd cover this part of the building," McCarter replied, disappointment in his voice. "But the bleedin' upstairs is deserted. Nothing here but empty beds and dusty furniture."

Katz, James and Hahn emerged from the clinic with Professor Casavska. The Phoenix Force commander gestured to Manning and McCarter to join them. The Canadian scooped up his air rifle and jogged toward the group. McCarter climbed over the windowsill and crept, sure-footed, along the ledge to a drainpipe. The Briton half climbed and half slid down the pipe to the ground.

The Phoenix Force team and Professor Casavska hurried to the gate. The beer truck driven by Alexei Cernak waited for them at the curb. The area was not in an urban setting, but a handful of bystanders watched from behind the safety of the windows of their homes. All these houses were somewhat less than a kilometer away. No one seemed too eager to get involved, although someone might have decided to call the police.

"You're early," Karl Hahn told Cernak as they climbed into the rear of the vehicle.

"Good thing I am," the Czech replied gruffly. "I heard shooting at least half a kilometer away. What went wrong?"

"We'll tell you all about it later," the German assured him. "Don't worry. It didn't really go badly at all."

"Sure," Cernak replied without enthusiasm as he shifted gears and pulled the truck away from the curb.

14

"Muluvite anglicky?" Karl Hahn asked Professor Casavska. *"Nebo nemecky?"*

"Ja," the scientist replied. *"Ich spreche deutsch."*

"Sehr gut," Hahn said, happily switching to his native tongue. "It'll be easier for us to communicate in German. Two of my friends also speak the language."

"Was sind Sie?" Casavska asked. "What are you? West German agents? If you think that the Czech government will pay a large ransom for me, I'm afraid you'll be disappointed. Prague doesn't have a very high opinion of me."

"You underestimate yourself," Yakov Katzenelenbogen commented. "The government appreciates your value. That's why they had you examine those corpses. Since you're one of the best nuclear specialists in Europe, I assume there was reason to believe that those men died from radiation poisoning of some sort. Correct?"

"You gentlemen must know that I was formerly in a reeducation center," Casavska remarked. "I was put there because I said things that made the government angry. However, don't misunderstand me. I am not a traitor to my country, nor do I have any desire to defect to West Germany or to the United States or whatever country you men represent. I refuse to help my own government or our allies in Moscow—at least that's what we're supposed to call them—construct more nuclear bombs and missiles. And I certainly won't agree to help the powers of the West in this monstrous arms race that can only lead to total destruction and death for all of us.''

"Professor," Gary Manning began. "We admire your courage and we respect your principles. We're not going to try to convince you to defect or attempt to smuggle you across the border. All we want are the answers to a few questions. Then we'll let you go."

"Ask what you like," Casavska replied wearily as he leaned against one of the wooden ribs of the truck frame. "That does not mean I'll answer you. You men have proved that you're very tough. You probably think you can beat information out of me. But I'm not as fragile as I appear. You will find that I do not break easily."

"We won't have to use such crude methods," Katz told him. "The black man who found you happens to be a trained medical man and a chemist. He's very skilled in the use of scopolamine. Are you familiar with this drug?"

"A very powerful truth serum," the professor said, nodding. "I happen to have a heart condition. Scopolamine would probably kill me. If that's what you want to do, frankly, I'd rather you used a bullet."

"Professor—" Katz sighed as he took a pack of Camels from his shirt pocket "—we have no desire to harm you, but we need information. There's too much at stake here. Too many lives are threatened for us to be terribly concerned about your life or about our own. If we have to, we'll use scopolamine, even if it kills you. We hope that won't be necessary, especially since your country is in greater danger than ours."

"Really?" Casavska raised his narrow eyebrows. "Would you be good enough to explain that statement?"

Katz told him everything they knew and suspected about the terrorists. He told Casavska about the United National German Party, Colonel Briggs and the World Army Freedom Network. The professor listened quietly and nodded twice.

"How do I know that you aren't connected with these terrorists?" Casavska inquired.

"If we were," Manning began, "why would we want to know if the men you examined had died from radiation poisoning? In fact, we'd probably already know more about it than you do."

"Incredible," the professor said, laughing. "I think you're telling me the truth. Even if you're not, I don't see that anything I can tell you would jeopardize national security. May I have one of those cigarettes?"

"Of course," Katz replied, handing him the Camels.

"American?" Casavska smiled. "I haven't smoked one of these for years. American cigarettes are wonderful."

Katz fired his Ronson lighter. Casavska poked the tip of the cigarette into the flame and drew smoke deep into his lungs. The scientist took another puff and flicked the ash onto the floorboards.

"All right," he began. "The bodies I examined were taken from the train wreck that occurred in the White Carpathians. That is true. However, the rumors of a chemical spill are incorrect. The dead men were Czech soldiers assigned to protect a special shipment of valuable merchandise that was stored in a special compartment in one of the cars."

"Uranium?" Hahn inquired, well aware that the potentially dangerous ore is found in Czechoslovakia.

"Very close," Casavska replied. "Plutonium 239, an extremely dangerous metal. It was being transported to a missile site where it would eventually wind up in the warheads of some of our new Mecoun missiles. At least that's what was planned for the plutonium."

"The train wreck was actually sabotage?" Manning asked.

"That's right," Casavska confirmed. "The saboteurs, who are probably connected with your terrorists, derailed the train. Then they stormed the storage car and stole the plutonium. They took less than ten kilos, but that's enough plutonium to destroy approximately eighty-five square kilometers and contaminate everything within a hundred and fifty kilometers beyond that. With a strong wind, the fallout could extend across borders into Germany, Austria or the Soviet Union."

"Jesus," Manning rasped. "Did the men guarding the plutonium die from exposure to it?"

"No," Casavska answered. "They were shot to death. I was called to determine if the bodies had been contaminated by any possible plutonium leaks. There was, in fact, an unusually high radiation level. That is why we had to use protective gear inside the clinic for the first twenty-four hours. However, after checking all of the bodies, I discovered that none of them had a dangerous radiation level on their skin. For the past few days, I've been testing for the internal effects of radiation poisoning."

"Internal?" Hahn frowned. "You mean certain forms of radiation affect only internal organs?"

"Not exactly," the Czech explained. "Certain forms affect *specific* parts of the anatomy. For example, iodine 131 assaults the thyroid gland. Now this is noticeable in a living person after a few days. It's also fatal unless treated. Actually, unless treatment is administered quickly enough, the person will die regardless of what you do for him."

"So you had to do an autopsy to search for this iodine... whatever," Manning mused.

"Oh, not just iodine 131," Casavska declared. "I did not find any evidence of that form of radiation poisoning, although I did find traces of strontium 90 in the bones of the corpses."

"Strontium 90?" Katz raised an eyebrow. "What does it do? Create something like bone cancer?"

"Very similar," the professor confirmed. "Strontium 90 destroys calcium and bone marrow. It is one of the worst forms of radiation poisoning. A terribly slow and painful way to die."

"Is it possible that the thieves who stole the plutonium will also become victims of strontium poisoning?" Hahn asked.

"Yes, unless they're very careful with that plutonium and keep it in a lead container." Casavska nodded. "It's like carrying around the head of Medusa. Only it would be more merciful to be turned to stone. I've made quite a study of plutonium diseases. That's why I'm opposed to nuclear weapons and fission reactors designed to produce additional plutonium."

"You're an odd nuclear physicist," Katz remarked. "You sound as if you'd be willing to put yourself out of a job."

"I'd like to see nuclear energy used solely for constructive purposes," Casavska answered. "We should be concentrating on developing fusion reactors. You see, fission is a violent process. Splitting atoms is very dangerous and very difficult to control. However, fusion welds nuclei, making a stable, heavier atom. It's the process that exists in nature. The sun is actually a giant fusion reactor."

"But the technology for nuclear fusion has not been perfected," Manning commented. "I seem to recall that it would require creating a source of heat that reaches ten million degrees."

"Theoretically," Casavska agreed. "Yet there might be other ways to create fusion. Ways that we haven't even imagined. Besides, it is now possible to create a million-degree temperature. The trick is to keep the enormous heat from burning through a vessel by using electromagnetic waves to prevent it from actually touching the walls...."

"That's all quite fascinating, Professor," Katz stated. "But our problem is finding the terrorists. Any advice?"

"If you learn of anyone suffering from strontium 90 poisoning, then you've found either a terrorist or a victim," Casavska said with a shrug. "And if that doesn't happen fairly soon, we've really got something to worry about. If these terrorists know how to handle plutonium, they might very well put together a nuclear weapon."

"Too true. You don't have to be a physicist to make a crude nuclear device," Manning said grimly. "It can be done with plastic explosives if the amount of plutonium is small enough."

"That's true," Casavska confirmed. "Of course, detonating the device at a safe distance might be a problem. One could build a makeshift rocket launcher, but assembling the parts would be difficult in Czechoslovakia. The authorities would quickly become suspicious of someone trying to obtain titanium tubing, chemicals for rocket fuel and radio detonators."

"Maybe that won't be a problem," Katz stated, his expression as solemn as that of a corpse. "I think we now have some idea why Briggs came across the border with those trucks."

"My God," Manning whispered. "He brought the components in a small-scale missile system with him. If his people can get the plutonium to him and make a warhead for one or more rockets, he'll be able to blow away a small city."

"With ten kilos of plutonium 239?" Casavska said. "He could blow away a *large* city. In fact, he could destroy *several* cities."

"Thanks for the information, Professor," Katz announced. "I think you've succeeded in scaring the hell out of us all."

"All except our friends who don't understand German," Hahn added, referring to McCarter and James. "I'm certain they'll be thrilled when we translate this discussion."

"In the meantime, let's drop the professor off on the outskirts of the next village," Katz continued. "Don't bother to memorize the license plate on this truck. It's a phony."

"Don't worry about that," Casavska assured them. "I'm not going to help the STB or the KGB hunt you down. Of course, I'll have to tell them some of what happened here."

"Please do," Katz invited. "Just try to make it clear to them how dangerous Briggs and his fanatics are. This is one time when the interests of the KGB and the STB are the same as our own."

"Not exactly," the professor said with a sigh. "I'm afraid they'll be as eager to get their hands on you as they will be to capture the terrorists."

"So what's new?" Manning replied with a shrug.

15

The farm was located in a valley on the Bohemian-Moravian Highlands. Hills and forests supplied natural camouflage for the men who had seized control of the property. The farm had belonged to an elderly Czech who had lived quietly with his wife and invalid brother far from the hectic pace of the cities and the depression and paranoia of a society fueled by tyrannical Communists. The farmer and his family might have lived out their remaining years in peace if the property had not been ideally suited for the needs of Colonel Briggs and his private army.

The farmer, his wife and brother were buried behind the farmhouse. Briggs and his followers had converted the place into a base of operations. The self-appointed colonel and his WAFN followers referred to it as Odin Three.

Herman Drache, the commander of the United German National Party, was not happy with the abrupt change in tactics that Briggs had decided to thrust upon him. Drache had been in charge of field operations in Czechoslovakia before Briggs had arrived to personally take command of the mission.

A physical-fitness enthusiast, Drache was a well-muscled man who kept in shape by weight lifting and kenpo karate. He believed that a sound body assisted a keen mind. Drache had been a bit reckless when he was younger. Stirring up the British Ku Klux Klan in London had been a mistake; he had been deported from England. The scandal had attracted a lot of attention and placed Drache in a spotlight of controversy.

The publicity had led to Drache's becoming a leader of the United German National Party. At first he had enjoyed the admiration, and relished making statements to the press about the threat of Communism, the hazards of liberalism and the conspiracies plotted by Jews, blacks and other ethnic groups. Yet Drache learned that this sort of behavior did not help sway the masses toward his beliefs.

He had decided that the best way to fight Communism was on the Communists' own turf. Drache was a gifted linguist and spoke Czechoslovakian fluently. He had studied the principles of espionage and terrorism. Drache had first persuaded Klaus Weiss to finance hit-and-run operations in Czechoslovakia. Drache had selected the men for the job and coordinated the attacks on Russian personnel. They had killed several KGB agents. Of course, many innocent lives had also been taken, but that is the nature of war. Better Czech lives than German lives, in Drache's opinion.

Drache had been satisfied with their progress, but Weiss and the American were impatient. They were also afraid of the West German authorities. It was time for them to lay low and wait for the heat to pass, but Briggs and Weiss had insisted upon a scheme that Drache regarded as stupid and far too risky.

The order to steal plutonium, at least six kilos, had astonished Drache. What the hell did they want plutonium for? Whatever the scheme was, it had to be Briggs's idea. The American colonel had always wanted to use nuclear weapons on someone—anyone. Whenever a country did something that upset Briggs, he wanted to turn it into a mushroom cloud.

Drache had gotten the plutonium for Briggs. The colonel had taken command of the operation and now Drache was second banana. Briggs had made quite a ceremony of this change of command. He praised Drache's patriotism and exceptional work. The colonel even awarded Drache with a gold-plated medal and a "field promotion" to lieutenant colonel.

"You'll be able to get a bit of rest now, soldier," Briggs told him with a smile. "I'll take the burden of command on my shoulders. Of course, I'll still be relying on you to be my strong right hand."

Drache thought Briggs needed a brain transplant more than a "strong right hand." The colonel's demand for plutonium was the beginning of a suicide mission. Briggs was insane, Drache had decided. That ridiculous cavalry charge across the border proved that the American had no intelligence. Drache felt as if he had been made second in command of a squad of kamikaze pilots.

Indeed, Briggs's leadership was already killing them. Drache grimly contemplated his fate and the fate of the men who had served as his agents for the past eight months within Czechoslovakia. During that time, none of Drache's men had been killed or captured.

Until now.

Twenty men had participated in the assault on the train transporting the plutonium to Czech missile sites. Five men had been killed during the brief gun battle with the soldiers guarding the radioactive material. Eight more had died after they delivered the plutonium to the farm. The seven men who remained were critically ill. So were four others who had handled the lead canister that held the plutonium.

Drache was saddened by the tragedy that had befallen his men. The German and American zealots had served under him with courage and loyalty. It angered Drache that his comrades had been forced to throw away their lives because Weiss and Briggs had decided to change operations from hit-and-run tactics to a crazy gamble with nuclear weapons.

The plutonium had been stored in a small grain silo, segregated from the UGNP and WAFN troops. When the men from the raid became sick, they, too, had to be segregated from the others. The stench of burned flesh hung in the air. Black smoke drifted from the large pit where the dead had to be cremated to prevent contamination from spreading throughout the camp.

Drache watched the bulky figures clad in silver suits as they shuffled from the silo. Their heads were covered with hoods, faces shielded by hard plastic windows. The resembled grotesque snowmen, animated shapes from a bizarre nightmare. The figures took turns spraying one another down with a chemical foam. They consulted a Geiger counter to check the radiation level of their suits and then began to strip off the protective gear.

"It's unfortunate your men did not use this sort of equipment during the raid," Colonel Briggs remarked as he ran a battery-powered razor along his cheeks and jaw. "Might have prevented this terrible tragedy."

"We didn't bring along any antiradiation suits," Drache replied grimly. "I suppose we should have foreseen the possibility that we'd be called upon to steal plutonium as part of our mission."

"Don't blame yourself, Drache," Briggs said in a soothing tone. The German's sarcasm had flown so high over the American's head that he had not even heard it flutter. "A good commander tries to prepare for everything, but no one is perfect. However, if anything like this occurs again, you might consider commandeering equipment from the enemy. When that isn't possible, try field expedience. Improvise. Some extra layers of clothing, heavy gloves and face masks might have saved the lives of your men."

"The plutonium was stored in lead, Colonel," Drache said, his teeth clenched with anger. "It was suppose to be safe to handle."

"Well—" Briggs sighed as he switched off his automatic razor and rubbed his face to inspect his shave "—it wasn't. Of course, that's all water over the dam now."

The four men who had left the silo finished stripping off their protective gear. Clad only in their shorts, they once again sprayed one another with the chemical foam. Another Geiger counter reading confirmed that the radiation level was low enough to allow them to safely approach the others. A dark-haired man with two fingers missing from his right hand stepped forward and saluted. Briggs returned the gesture.

"Colonel Drache, this is Captain Heywood," Briggs told his second in command. "The captain is an expert in nuclear radiation and weaponry. He was formerly an officer in the United States Navy and served on board a nuclear submarine. Please report, Captain."

"The original lead case containing the plutonium was cracked, sir," Heywood declared. "That's how the leak occurred and how the men involved in the raid received radiation poisoning. Plutonium is the most dangerous form of radioactive material. One little mistake can be fatal."

"I understand, Captain," Briggs replied. "Is the plutonium in a safe container now?"

"Yes, sir," Heywood confirmed. "It's now in a very thick, double-strength lead container. It's been broken into sections that in turn will be stored in separate lead cases. Thus when it becomes time to put the material in the warheads, we'll be able to do so with minimum safety equipment."

"Good work, Captain," Briggs said with a nod. "Did you check on the soldiers in sick bay?"

"Yes, sir," Heywood answered with a sigh. "I'm afraid there was nothing I could do for any of them. Perhaps if we'd known what sort of radiation poisoning they were suffering from, it would have been different—"

"Would have been?" Drache interrupted sharply. "What did you do to those men?"

"What had to be done, sir," the captain answered.

"You killed them!" Drache snarled, his hand streaking to the Walther PPK tucked in the holster under his left arm.

"Nein!" Briggs ordered, quickly stepping between Drache and Heywood. "The captain was acting on my orders. I told him that if there wasn't any reasonble hope of assisting those poor wretches, then he was to put them out of their misery."

"They were my men, damn you!" Drache snapped. He was tempted to use his pistol on the American colonel, but realized this would be suicidal.

"They were my men, too, Drache," Briggs told him. "Don't you think I care about the lives of my people? That's why I ordered Heywood to terminate them. It was the only merciful thing to do. Think of it, Drache. Wasting away in agony, slowly dying from radiation poisoning. Wouldn't you prefer a rapid, relatively painless death to such a terrible fate?"

"How did you do it, Captain?" Drache asked, his anger subsiding at last.

"A canister of cyanide gas," Heywood answered. "Very quick and almost painless."

"How do you know?" Drache snorted. "Have you ever taken a lethal does of cyanide gas, Captain?"

"Come now, Drache," Briggs scolded. "Don't give the captain a hard time. He was simply following orders. I'll want a list of the names of all the men who died in the process of obtaining plutonium for us. When this mission is completed, I intend to have a monument erected in their honor. They were heroes, every one of them. Their sacrifice will not be in vain."

"Of course," Drache said glumly. "I'm sure they'd appreciate such a gesture, Colonel."

"I agree," Briggs said with a nod, again failing to notice Drache's sarcasm. "And it won't be long before we've claimed the greatest victory for the political West of the twentieth century. We will go down in history as the force that drove Communism from Czechoslovakia and conquered it in the name of freedom."

"Freedom," Drache said with a nod. He wondered if anyone still knew what the word meant. Indeed, did anyone still care?

16

"Dekuji, Tovarisch Casavska," Captain Mikail Ivanovich Renkov told Professor Casavska. "Thank you, Comrade. Your story was most interesting."

"It is also true, Captain," Casavska assured him as he rose from a chair in the lobby of the Jaroslav Heyrovsky Clinic. "I urge you to consider the seriousness of—"

"I believe you have work to do, Professor," the KGB officer declared gruffly. "Please do not try to tell me how to do mine. That will be all, Professor. *Na shledanou.*"

Major Ladislav Svoboda watched Professor Casavska leave the room. The STB case officer glanced over his notes as Renkov took a silver-plated cigarette case from his jacket. The Tatar turned to Svoboda and put a short black cigarette in his toadlike mouth.

"Well, Major," Renkov began. "What do you think?"

"I think the professor told us the truth," Svoboda replied.

"More or less," Renkov agreed. "Although I don't believe those five butchers told him the truth. You will recall, I warned you about those gangsters. As soon as I learned five special commandos connected to the United States were active in West Germany, I knew they had to be involved in this terrorist mess, as well."

"Then you don't believe they're trying to stop the terrorists?" the STB agent inquired.

"Of course not," the Tatar scoffed. "That was propoganda they fed to that gullible fool Casavska. They're hoping he'll spread their lies to more would-be subversives. Don't forget, the professor is hardly a Czech patriot."

"He's not exactly a subversive, either," Svoboda said with a shrug. "After all, Casavska didn't offer to defect. In fact, he told them he wouldn't. Since he's probably going back to the rehabilitation center for more KGB 'behavior-modification treatment,' I'd say he must love his country very much to still want to stay here."

"Are your criticizing our program, Major?" Renkov blared at Svoboda.

"Not at all," the Czech intel agent replied smoothly. "In fact, I think Casavska is a splendid example of how well our Soviet comrades' rehabilitation system works. It is truly an epic accomplishment when a disgruntled rabble-rouser like Casavska can become a responsible member of society after only a few months of special education."

"I'm so glad you approve of it, Major," Renkov replied.

"Of course," Svoboda continued. "This adds more credibility to the professor's statement."

"Da!" the KGB man said sharply, pointing at Svoboda with the lit end of his cigarette. "Of the professor's statement, *not* of the five gangsters."

"But why wouldn't these hoodlums simply slaughter all the guards during the raid," the Czech remarked.

"In case you failed to notice, half a dozen of your countrymen were carried out of here with sheets over their heads," Renkov said grimly.

"Five men," Svoboda said with a nod. "However, three times as many were simply rendered unconscious. Why did the gangsters use sleep darts and electrical stunning devices instead of silenced weapons and garrotes? The terrorist actions beforc showed no signs of compassion or concern for human life. Why did these five take such trouble to spare the lives of so many?''

"Propaganda for Casavska again," Renkov declared.

"Maybe," the STB agent allowed. "But I think it would be a mistake to concentrate on these five men and fail to follow up on any other leads concerning the terrorists.''

"Investigate any possible evidence that you can find," Renkov invited. "But don't dismiss what happened here and don't start to admire those capitalist thugs. Remember what side you're on, Comrade.''

"Don't worry about that," Svoboda assured him. "I am totally dedicated to fighting the enemies of my country. That includes these five supercommandos.''

"They're not supermen," Renkov corrected. "They'll die when bullets are pumped into their bodies. And that's exactly what I want done to them when we find those bastards. They're too dangerous to try to take them alive. They are to be shot on sight. Do I make myself clear, Major?''

"Like Moser crystal," Svoboda confirmed.

FAROSLAV ZATOPEK WAS WORRIED. The Czech buried his shaggy head in his hands and groaned after listening to Phoenix Force explain what happened during the raid on the Heyrovsky Clinic. He was obviously less than pleased by the boldness of his "guests." The five commandos and Alexei Cernak sat in the basement safe house beneath Zatopek's auto-repair shop and waited for their host to speak.

"Was tun Sie?" Zatopek demanded, remembering to speak German instead of Czech. "What are you doing? Trying to cause more trouble than we already had?''

"We needed information, Herr Zatopek," Karl Hahn replied.

"Information?" Zatopek rolled his eyes. "I am familiar with the process required to gather information. One either observes or contacts others who have observed matters that one wishes to know about. One asks questions. One might eavesdrop or plant a microphone in an office or a bathroom. But charging into a state clinic, shooting up the place and kidnapping a noted nuclear scientist is not gathering information. It is insanity!''

''Gathering intelligence is generally done over a period of time,'' Katz agreed. ''But time is something we've got precious little of, my friend.''

''When you told us about Professor Casavska we had to take action,'' Gary Manning added. ''And what we learned confirmed that the situation is even worse than we thought it was when we accepted this mission.''

''I know,'' Zatopek said. ''You told me about the plutonium. These terrorists are going to blow up the entire country of Czechoslovakia? That seems pretty farfetched to me.''

''Well, they didn't steal that plutonium to recharge the batteries in their transistor radios,'' Hahn said dryly.

''I have no doubt that's what they intend to do with the stuff,'' the Czech assured him. ''But didn't Casavska say the container had leaked poisonous radiation? The terrorists who stole that plutonium are probably dead by now. Their comrades will certainly have given up the idea of using such deadly material. I wouldn't be surprised if they've fled across the border and given up their crazy schemes.''

''I doubt that's happened, Herr Zatopek,'' Katz said grimly. ''Perhaps you're right about the terrorists who actually stole the plutonium. They may be dead, but I don't think that will stop Colonel Briggs and the other fanatics. They brought trucks across the border. Why?''

''We've discussed this before.'' Zatopek sighed. ''They must have brought men and weapons....''

''WAFN and the UGNP have managed to smuggle agents into Czechoslovakia in the past,'' Hahn insisted. ''How do you think they got people into Czechoslovakia to commit acts of terrorism before Briggs arrived? They didn't have to smash through a fence in order to infiltrate your country. There had to be something else in that truck. Something that was too bulky to carry across the border any other way.''

"Such as?" Zatopek inquired.

"Lead shields and vessels to store plutonium," Gary Manning answered. "Probably protective suits, Geiger counters, decontamination equipment and whatever else they'd need to handle the plutonium."

"And some type of rockets and the equipment for launching them," Hahn added.

"Rockets?" Zatopek scoffed. "I don't claim to know much about nuclear weaponry, but I do know that's complicated. A bunch of fanatics couldn't build a nuclear missile and launch it. That would require a physicist and experts in rocketry...."

"If we were talking about a sophisticated guided missile such as those used by major governments, yes," Manning told him. "But we're dealing with men who intend to use these weapons within the country. They don't need to launch the projectiles across borders thousands of kilometers away. They don't have to worry about radar, antiballistic missiles or other detection devices. The missiles will be launched from such close range that no security device would be able to stop them, and there will be no time to run to bomb shelters."

"But the technology involved . . ." Zatopek insisted.

"Would be no more complex than that of a rather advanced model airplane operated by radio remote control," Hahn stated. "I could put such a system together and Mr. Summer could conjure up the explosives necessary to detonate a small amount of plutonium."

"Which one of you claims to be Summer?" Zatopek asked.

"That's me," Manning answered. "And exploding a small nuclear device isn't that difficult. In fact, it's terrifyingly simple. If you have some plutonium, some paraffin wax or other substance to retain neutrons, a metal sphere—even aluminum foil will do—and enough plastique, you can make a perfectly lethal, if rather crude, nuclear weapon."

"And how much damage would such a 'crude weapon' cause?" the horrified Czech inquired.

"Between one to four square kilometers will be destroyed," Manning answered. "Lesser damage will occur up to twice that distance. Fallout is another factor. It's unpredictable, depending on the size of the explosion, potency of the plutonium and wind currents."

"My God," Zatopek whispered. "Why hasn't something like this happened already?"

"Because we've been lucky," Katz answered. "Considering the suicidal nature of certain terrorist groups, such as the Japanese Red Army, the Shi'ite Muslim extremists and others, it's a minor miracle someone hasn't used a homemade nuclear weapon for terrorist purposes."

"The difficult part must be obtaining the plutonium," Alexei Cernak remarked. "Fortunately robberies such as the one that occurred at the train must be very rare."

"Not as rare as you might think," Manning said grimly. "Officially there are close to two tons of plutonium missing in the United States alone. It's estimated there are close to ten metric tons of plutonium unaccounted for throughout the world and more than fifty million tons of uranium."

"That's terrifying," Zatopek gasped.

"Certainly is," Hahn agreed. "But our immediate problem is how to deal with Briggs and his gang."

"How can you hope to find them in time?" Zatopek asked.

"The only thing we can do right now is try to acquire more information," Katz explained. "Faroslav, you and Alexei will have to contact your sources. Any information about foreigners trying to keep a low profile, strangers purchasing weapons or explosives from black marketeers, anything of that nature. Also, if any medical centers are robbed of supplies that might be used to treat someone with radiation sickness."

"How will they know what sort of medicines that would be?" Cernak inquired.

"Mr. Walker?" Katz called to Calvin James.

"Hey, they're talking to one of us," David McCarter said with mock astonishment. The Briton and Calvin James had been sitting apart from the others, unable to participate in the conversation since neither men understood German.

"I think he's talking to me," James commented, placing a hand over his heart. "Yes, Mr. Warburg, I hear you."

"We'll need a list of medicines and chemicals that would be used to treat a person suffering from radiation poisoning."

"Okay," the black warrior said with a shrug. "But I figure it's a waste of time. Briggs will probably treat his wounded with a bullet in the head, man."

"You're probably right," Katz admitted. "We have to check every possibility, anyway. Please make the list."

"Sure," James said with a nod. "That'll give me something to do while you guys chat away in German."

"Is there anything I can do?" McCarter inquired. "I'm getting so bloody bored I'm ready to take up knitting."

"I could use a new turtleneck, thanks," Gary Manning told the Briton.

"You can nail that map of Prague to the wall, Mr. St. John," Katz instructed. "Unless you'd rather go out and buy some yarn."

"How droll," McCarter muttered as he unrolled a street map of Prague and picked up a hammer.

"You believe the terorrists will strike in Prague?" Cernak inquired, watching the Briton nail the map into place.

"It's the logical target," Karl Hahn answered. "Prague is the capital of Czechoslovakia and the center of your government."

"Correction," Cernak said with a sigh. "Moscow is the real center of our government."

"Yeah," Manning agreed. "But the Kremlin is too far away."

"Now," Katz began as he approached the map. "Correct me if I'm wrong. The president of the republic resides at the old Prague Castle in Lesser Town."

"We call it the 'Hradcany,'" Cernak confirmed. "Of course, the main power resides with the Central Committee and the Party Congress. Then there's the Federal Assembly, comprised of the House of the People and the House of Nations. It determines most of our domestic and foreign policies."

"That's another likely target," Katz agreed. "Although the Hradcany would make more of an impression. Look at where it's located. A missile explosion there would wipe out the castle, the National Gallery, St. Vitus's Cathedral and Stembeck Palace."

"They've probably got more than one rocket," Hahn said. "That means they can strike at more than one target."

"And I think I know where one of those targets will be," Manning stated as he stepped forward and thrust a finger at the map. "Here in Mala Strana, Lesser Town, not far from Prague Castle, but far enough away to merit another missile."

"The Soviet Embassy," Katz said, nodding. "I agree, Mr Summer. I also think it's possible, if they have enough pluonium and missiles, that the terrorists might launch rockets at the Soviet 103rd Armored Division about seven kilometers south of Prague.''

"They'll probably need more than one launching system for that," Hahn remarked. "We'd better concentrate on finding a rocket base in Mala Strana or close to that area."

"Do you think they've already set up for the missile strike?" Cernak asked, a slight quiver in his voice.

"It's possible," Manning replied. "But I think they'll need time to get the missiles ready and move them into position. How much time will depend on the number of men in Briggs's group and how well they've been trained to handle something like this. We'd be kidding ourselves if we thought we had more than a day or two."

"Well, gentlemen," Katz declared. "I have a feeling none of us will be getting much sleep over the next forty-eight hours. We'd better sleep in shifts until this mission is over."

"How can any of us get any sleep when we know a bunch of lunatics might set off plutonium bombs any second now?" Cernak asked.

"We might as well try to get some sleep," Karl Hahn replied with a shrug. "After all, we're already in the middle of a nightmare."

17

Colonel Zackery Briggs drew deeply on a cheroot as he watched his men load the last section of sewer pipe onto the platform of a large flatbed trailer. The WAFN and UGNP members had to struggle with the big concrete tubing. Each section was fifteen feet long and weighed almost one metric ton. The men were equipped with only a diesel-powered crane and chains to haul the heavy pipes onto the flatbed.

Hijacking the truck had been a stroke of genius in Briggs's estimation. Naturally it had been his idea. The huge pipes were ideal hiding places for the equipment. With chains and locks to brace the pipes, the method was a secure one for smuggling their gear into Prague. The rig would not attract any suspicion and the original driver could not report the hijacking. One of Briggs's flunkies had strangled the man with a wire garrote.

The pipes were more than large enough to conceal the four six-foot-long aluminum-and-plastic rockets and the guidance-system control panel. Three reinforced lead cases were fitted inside three separate pipes. Canvas padding had been added to ensure that the containers did not get bounced about and damaged during transport.

The lead shields and other protective gear were placed in the back of a battered old pickup truck that had belonged to the farmer that Briggs's men had murdered. The material was covered with a mound of sand to conceal the items in the event of a standard search. Of course, Briggs and his men had been forced to abandon the trucks and the jeep they had used to crash their way into Czechoslovakia. They would commandeer other means of transportation to get the men to Prague.

Some of the troops were already in the city. They would prepare the site for the missile setup. Others would enter Prague on motorcycle, moped and bicycle. The rest would be disguised as factory workers and loaded in a truck to be driven by Herman Drache.

The men who were already in the city did not know the details of Briggs's plan. However, the Americans and Germans who had loaded the trucks at the farmhouse were aware of the plutonium and of the large number of lives that had already been lost during the mission. Some would have already guessed what Briggs intended to do. The colonel had therefore decided it was time to brief the men on tomorrow's mission.

"Colonel Drache," Briggs began. "Will you be good enough to translate my speech into German for the sake of those members of the UGNP who do not understand English?"

"Of course, Colonel," Drache agreed as he approached the American zealot. He turned to the troops. *"Meine Herren! Kommen Sie hier, bitte!"*

The men gathered around the two commanders. The members of the World Army Freedom Network and the United German National Party were all extremists, but they varied from hate-filled racists and kill-crazy psychos to misguided reactionaries. The former were homicidal savages who had found a "cause" to justify their bloodlust. The latter were frightened men who felt international conspiracies were closing in on them from all sides. They associated patriotism with fighting Communism and found the philosophies of paramilitary groups appealing. They were too quick to believe anything and everything spoken by a flag-waving warmonger.

"We've all been tested during the past two days," Colonel Briggs began. "Many of our comrades at arms have laid down their lives for our cause. We've fought shoulder to shoulder against the enemy, and tomorrow we must be prepared to make the ultimate sacrifice."

Briggs puffed up his chest proudly as he scanned the faces of his followers. Together they would claim the greatest victory since Napoleon had conquered half of Europe.

"Our fate will be in the hands of God," Briggs declared. "Unlike these Commie atheists, we have a God. As the Lord Jesus gave His life to save our souls, so too may some of us be called upon to give our lives in the fight for freedom. I want you all to be prepared to die, although I believe tomorrow will be the final phase of our mission and I predict total success with little—if any—bloodshed."

"Here—" the colonel waved a hand toward the sewer pipes mounted on the flatbed "—here is one of the most formidable weapons known to man. You all know about the plutonium and the missiles we've packed inside these pipes. We are going to do what the gutless governments of the West should have done long ago. We're going to use nuclear muscle to expose the Communists for the cowards they truly are. I promised you we'd overthrow the Reds and establish Czechoslovakia as the first iron-curtain country to be freed from the constraints of Communism."

Briggs smiled as he continued. "And that will be just the beginning," he declared. "When we set the example, more brave men will rally behind us. We'll liberate East Germany and Hungary. One by one, the Soviet Union will lose power in these countries until nothing remains of its reign except a bad memory. And then we'll march into Moscow."

Voices mumbled in the crowd. Some sounded excited, but others seemed distressed. No one openly criticized his commander's plan.

"Some of you are probably wondering what will happen if the Commies don't back down?" Briggs remarked, aware of the apprehension that many of his people were feeling. "I've studied the Russkies for a long time. The average Russian is a coward. They're an inferior lot. Liars, weaklings and cowards. Throughout history, they've often backed down when somebody pushed them. That's why the Japs whipped their asses in 1905. That's why Hitler marched right in and thumped Russkie heads during the Second World War. That's why they backed down during the Cuban Missile Crisis. They don't have any balls. The bastards have no stomach for a real fight."

Colonel Briggs's history lesson had little to do with reality. The Russo-Japanese War had consisted of naval battles that the Russians had not been prepared to wage at that particular time. The Russian front was regarded with terror by the Nazis during World War II and the Soviet people fought like wildcats against Hitler's minions. However, Briggs was using a tactic popular among propaganda peddlers and hate-mongers.

Belittling the opposition is meant to instill confidence in the troops. Briggs believed that it is also easier to kill people when you regard them as inferior. He used the term "Russkie" in the same manner as Adolf Hitler might have used *Schweine Jude*. He wanted his men to be certain they were better than the Russian or Czechoslovakian vermin. He wanted them to be as confident of success as he was.

"When we arrive in Prague," Briggs continued, "we will seize control of the main railroad station at Vitezneho Unora. There we will set up the missile system and contact the Presidium and the Soviet Embassy via telephone to make our demands. The Czech government will do whatever the Russkies tell them to do. The great Russian bear has a big yellow streak down its back. When they learn we have weapons loaded with plutonium and that we're prepared to blast them to hell and blanket the city with radioactive fall-out, they will surrender.''

Drache translated Briggs's words, keeping the inflection of his voice neutral. The German and American terrorists stared at Colonel Briggs. They had been fully aware of the plutonium missiles, but they had not known the details of the mission until that moment. Some were excited by the proposed confrontation. Others were stunned and frightened by the plan.

''Excuse me, Colonel,'' an American named Michael Baker spoke up. ''May I ask a question, sir?''

''Very well, Sergeant,'' Briggs replied with a curt nod.

''Well, sir,'' Baker said awkwardly. ''What . . . what will happen if the Communists don't surrender to our demands?''

''One never makes hollow threats, Sergeant Baker,'' the colonel declared. ''If the Russians call our bluff, we'll have to show them we mean business. The missiles will be launched. What other choice would we have? The KGB would torture us if they took us captive. I'm sure you've all heard about their methods.''

''Sir?'' a German terrorist began in broken English. ''Suicide is not good idea with me. *Ja?* Is there not some way the missiles can be used without us all die?''

''Fuckin' coward!'' a voice with a deep Alabama drawl snorted. ''You sure you're a German, Schuller? You're soundin' as gutless as a gawddamn Russkie to me.''

''I am not coward,'' Schuller insisted. ''But I not want to die if it is not necessary. Do you? Do any . . . does anybody want to die if there is other way?''

''Herr Schuller,'' Briggs began, unfamiliar with the man and unaware of his rank in the UGNP. ''We wouldn't have time to safely get away after launching the missiles. The explosions will destroy everything within a four- or five-mile radius. Is that accurate, Captain Heywood?"

"Oh, at least that much, sir," the Captain confirmed. "Our deaths will be instantaneous. That's better than being smashed about by the blast beyond ground zero. The effects would then be similar to a serious automobile accident. Radiation poisoning would set in. You all saw what a terrible way to die that can be. Trust me. It's better to take the express to the next world than die the way they did."

"The captain's right," another voice agreed. "I seen how those fellas suffered and I ain't gonna go that way if I can help it."

"At ease!" Colonel Briggs snapped. His tone clearly indicated that he was using the term as the military equivalent of "shut up."

"Halt's Maul!" Drache barked the translation.

"Danke, Colonel Drache," Briggs said before he addressed the troops once more. "All of you men knew there was an element of risk involved in this mission. True, that element might increase when we reach Prague. Yet I am positive we shall succeed. Even if we die, our sacrifice will certainly be an encouragement to men of freedom and courage throughout the world. This is the chance of a lifetime. Anyone who does not wish to participate should step aside now. I don't want him polluting the air of the rest of you brave men."

Five UGNP and three WAFN members stepped from the formation. Schuller began to join them, but Sergeant Baker caught his sleeve. The German almost pulled his arm free. Baker leaned forward and whispered softly.

"Don't play his game, man," the American warned. "Briggs likes to stack the deck. *Verstehen?"*

Schuller did not understand what Baker meant, but he decided not to step aside. The others moved away from the eight men who wanted out of the mission. Other members of the assault force probably wanted to bow out, as well. Yet because of pride, the fear of losing face and the stigma of cowardice they stayed. A few knew Colonel Briggs well enough to suspect he would deal harshly with anyone who dared to undermine the mission.

"Eight of you, eh?" Briggs said dryly. "Well, I'm glad you were honest enough to admit that you're cowards. I suppose that gives you one virtue. Actually, I don't really object. I wouldn't want you to participate in this mission if you really didn't want to."

Briggs gestured at four of his most trusted WAFN members. They had been with the colonel for many years, long enough to prove their total dedication to WAFN and to Zackery Briggs. The four flunkies snapped to attention.

"For security reasons," Briggs began, "I'm forced to have you eight men placed under arrest and held in detention. You will surrender your weapons to these four soldiers."

"But, sir..." one of the eight men began.

"Just do it!" Briggs snapped. "If any one of you tries to resist, the guards will kill all eight of you. I hope that's understood."

"We understand, Colonel," one of the four guards said with a smile.

"I thought so," Briggs replied. "The rest of you men will fall out from formation and get some rest. We will be leaving just before dawn, so get as much sleep as possible. Good night, gentlemen, and thank you."

The majority of the men walked to their bivouac area, while the remaining eight raised their hands. The four watchdogs aimed submachine guns at the prisoners and ordered them to turn around. Schuller glanced over his shoulder and cursed under his breath.

"I think we'd better talk about this," Sergeant Baker whispered to the German.

"Talk?" Schuller replied softly. "What good will that be? Need we more than for talking to get out from this *scheisser*."

"Your English sucks, pal," Baker commented.

"Thank you," Schuller answered. "Work I on my English a lot."

The sudden eruption on full-auto fire drew their attention to the eight prisoners and their keepers. The guards had opened fire on the captives. Sparks of flame spat form the muzzles of subguns through the shadows. The eight targets screamed as bullets slammed into their flesh. They toppled to the ground as the four gunmen stepped closer and blasted another volley to make certain that none of their prisoners would ever get up again.

"A couple of the bastards tried to pull guns on us!" a guard shouted. "We had to kill 'em, Colonel!"

"That's all right, Master Sergeant Colby," Briggs replied. "Get a burial detail together and get those traitors out of my sight as soon as possible."

"Now do you see why I wanted you to stay put when we were in formation?" Baker remarked to Schuller.

"*Ja,*" the German said with a nod. "*Danke, Herr Feldwebel.*"

"The name's Baker, not Feltball."

"*Feldwebel* means sergeant," Schuller explained.

"Fuck that," the American snorted. "Just call me 'Baker.' Look, Schuller. We've gotta get out of hcrc. Briggs is nuts. He's gonna get us all killed. Personally, I don't give a shit if we take most of Czechoslovakia with us. Christ, this country never did anything to me."

"What do we, then?" Schuller asked. "Warn the Czechs?"

"If we have to," Baker answered. "Hell, even if Briggs is right about the government surrendering and the Soviet Embassy agreeing to pull out, the Russians won't let us get away with this. Shit, Moscow will probably launch a couple of missiles five minutes after the coup."

"You are right, Baker," Schuller agreed. "But first we must go from here. I know a friend who can help."

"You sure we can trust him?"

"Have we a choice?"

"Not much," Baker admitted. "But remember, most of these guys are as crazy as Briggs. Trust the wrong joker and we'll wind up like those dumb bastards who were just shot 'trying to resist arrest.'"

Schuller raised his eyebrows. "Oh, *nein*, Baker. I mean not a friend here in the group. He is in Pisek."

"Where the hell is that?"

"Ten kilometers, maybe," Schuller said with a shrug. A little more, maybe. Closer it is than Prague. My friend is in the underground, resisting Communists."

"I just hope he's got enough sense to help us," Baker remarked as he glanced about. "You know, right now might be the best time to make a break. Everybody is still preoccupied with the shootings. Nobody's watching us and Briggs hasn't posted any sentries yet. You can bet he will try to stop anybody else from trying to go AWOL during the night."

"Then we go now," Schuller agreed with a nod.

The pair quietly moved to the edge of the camp and melted into the shadows. They took advantage of the darkness and natural cover of the surrounding forest. Out of sight of the farm, the pair broke into a run. At any moment they expected to hear Briggs's troops chasing them. Yet the sounds of footfalls, shouts and gunshots did not occur.

"By God," Baker said breathlessly as he leaned against a tree trunk and gazed at the silent woods. "I think we're gonna make it."

"Not if stand we still and talk," Schuller insisted. "Keep moving. *Ja?*"

"Ja," Baker agreed. "Let's haul ass."

"Hole as?" the confused Schuller inquired, but he did not waste time asking for explanations when Baker jogged deeper into the woods. The German breathed deeply and hurried after his American ally.

18

"My friends, our prayers have been answered," Alexei Cernak announced as he descended the ladder to the basement safe house where the members of Phoenix Force were waiting. A contact of mine in Pislek has news for us."

"What sort of news, Alexei?" Karl Hahn asked.

"He's bringing us two defectors from Colonel Briggs's private army," the Czech replied cheerfully. "One German and one American. The German is a fellow named Horst Schuller. He used to work with a cutout group that specialized in helping Czechs escape into West Germany. I met him once. Not really a bad sort..."

"Give us his biography later," Katz interrupted. "Where are these defectors?"

"I told you," Cernak said with a shrug. "They're on their way here. Bedrich Fanacek—he's my contact in Pislek—is bringing them to Pizen so we can talk with them."

"He's not bringing them to the auto shop, is he?" Gary Manning asked as he reached for his jacket. "That would be too risky for our friend Zatopek."

"You're right," Cernak agreed with the Canadian. "We'll meet with them at a rendezvous point outside of town."

"Shit," Calvin James commented. "We'd better get moving. When are these dudes due to arrive?"

"In about half an hour," Cernak answered, glancing at his wristwatch. "It is now 3:35 A.M. Fanacek and the defectors should be at the rendezvous point at 4:00 A.M. on the nose. Is that the correct expression?"

"Load your weapons," Katz told the other members of Phoenix Force. "We might not have time to come back and get them later. If these characters really are defectors, Briggs might realize they've gone AWOL by now. Judging from what happened at the Weiss estate, Briggs has a habit of responding to a threat by jumping ahead of schedule in order to carry out a mission. As soon as we talk to these guys, we might have to move and move fast."

"Thank God," David McCarter muttered. "I could die of bloody boredom hanging around this place."

"You might die of something else when we catch up with Briggs and his gang," Manning remarked, gathering up a canvas bag that contained his gear.

"I know damn good and well I'll die in combat, mate," the Briton replied with a grin. "That's probably how we're all going to die, anyway. Beats the hell out of a retirement home."

"Yeah," James commented as he checked his Jackass Leather shoulder-holster rig with the holstered Colt Commander under his left arm and a G-96 dagger sheathed under his right. "But we'd better get moving, or Prague might go up in a mushroom cloud."

Phoenix Force climbed into the back of a milk truck. The vehicle, actually a van, belonged to a state-owned dairy company. However, the government allowed each branch to manage its section with little interference. Local companies were allowed to determine salaries for personnel, providing these were neither excessively higher or lower than state standards, and it even permitted the companies to pay bonuses to individuals with exceptional work records. These were practices of "creeping capitalism," but the Czech economy had clearly benefited from such policies. Even a hard-core Communist has trouble finding fault with success.

The manager of the milk company in Pizen was a friend of Alexei Cernak. He had agreed to "loan" one of his trucks to Cernak. If the vehicle was not returned by 7:00 A.M. the manager would report it stolen.

Cernak drove the milk van beyond the city limits of Pizen and pulled onto a dirt road. A battered old pickup truck was parked at the shoulder of the road, its hood raised. A lone figure, dressed in a coat and hat, stood by the vehicle with flashlight in hand. Cernak pulled up to the truck and brought the milk van to a halt.

"Dobry vecer," Cernak greeted the figure. *"Zabloudil jsem. Muzete mi pomoci?"*

"Mozna," the man with the flashlight replied as he approached the van. *"Pomozte mi vymenit pneumatiku, prosim?"*

"What are they saying?" Calvin James whispered the question to Karl Hahn as they huddled in the back of the milk van.

"Alexei claimed he was lost and asked for directions, and the other guy asked for help fixing his tire," Hahn answered.

"Thought they knew each other," McCarter remarked, reaching for his canvas bag to grab his Ingram M-10 machine pistol.

"It's dark," Katz stated. "And Alexei just wants to make sure who it is. Don't jump to any conclusions just yet."

"All right, my friends!" Cernak's voice called out. "You can come out. Everything is okay."

Phoenix Force climbed from the rear of the milk truck. Cernak introduced them to Bedrich Fanacek. A middle-aged man with a sad face and a weak smile greeted the commandos. Schuller and Baker emerged from a pile of grain sacks

n the back of the pickup. They nervously approached the
nen of Phoenix Force.

"So these are our defectors from Colonel Briggs's merry
•and of terrorists," Gary Manning remarked.

"We're not terrorists," Baker replied.

"The United German National Party and the World
Army Freedom Network have killed a lot of innocent peo-
•le all over Czechoslovakia and it looks as though Briggs is
•lanning to blackmail the Communists with plutonium
veapons," Katz stated. "If that's not terrorism, what is
t?"

"How did you know about the plutonium?" Baker asked
n astonishment.

"Never mind," McCarter said gruffly. "Just answer our
•leeding questions. Where is Briggs?"

"We want promise from you that we go not to jail,"
Schuller insisted. "Is fair. *Ja?*"

"If you help us you've got nothing to be afraid of," Katz
assured them. "Now tell us about Briggs. Where is he,
what's he planning and how many men does he have?"

"Briggs has a camp at a farmhouse in the Bohemian
Forest," Baker answered.

"Nein," Schuller declared. "On the Bohemian-Moravian
Highlands."

"Well, which is it?" James demanded.

"Schuller's probably right," Baker said with a shrug.
'He knows this fuckin' country a lot better than I do.
Doesn't make much of a difference, anyway. Briggs is gonna
strike camp and hit the road before dawn. They're probably packing up their stuff and heading for Prague right
now. You'll never catch 'em at the farm."

"We figured they'd pick Prague for their target," Karl
Hahn said. "Exactly when are they planning the operation
and where will they set up the missiles?"

"Shortly after dawn, I guess," Baker answered. "Briggs said some of his men were already in Prague. They're supposed to seize control of some railroad station."

"The main station at Vitezneho Unora," Schuller added.

"That's in Nove Mesto," Hahn remarked with a frown. "New Town. We guessed they'd set up in Lower Town so they could take aim at Prague Castle and the Soviet Embassy."

"Those are the targets," Baker told him. "Maybe they can get a better shot from the train station or something."

"New Town is on the opposite side of the city," Hahn stated. "I guess whoever put together their rockets must be awfully confident of his guidance system."

"Maybe Briggs and his boys are dumb enough to think they'll be far enough from the blast not to get killed," Manning commented.

"Nein, Mein Herr," Schuller announced. "Briggs told everyone they would quickly die if the missiles exploded. Of course, he believes the Communists will surrender to him."

"He's crazy," James muttered. "How the hell did he get so many of you dudes to go along with this stupid shit?"

"We're opposed to Communism," Baker replied. "We thought we could strike a blow for freedom."

"By blowing up a bunch of people?" The black commando glared at him. "Even if his scheme works, he won't be liberating Czechoslovakia. What does he plan to replace the Communist government with?"

"He didn't talk about that much," Baker admitted. "Said we'd have to enforce martial law at first."

"In other words a military dictatorship with him in charge," Manning commented. "Some blow for freedom. The WAFN and UGNP want to goose-step through the steets of Prague so the Czechs can tremble to the sound of their jackboots instead of the Russians'."

"The hell with what Briggs plans to do or why," Mc-Carter snorted. "Let's just make certain none of his dreams come true."

"How many men does Briggs have?" Katz asked.

"Nobody knows for sure," Baker replied. "A bunch of guys were killed by radiation poisoning. Mostly UGNP. They were working for Herman Drache before Briggs showed up."

"So Drache's in Czechoslovakia, too," Hahn mused. "Look, we don't care about the men who are dead. How many live opponents are left?"

"Well, they executed eight guys last night and Schuller and I went AWOL," Baker mused. "Guess that leaves about fifteen or sixteen guys at the farm. But don't forget, they've already got agents in Prague. Better figure on at least thirty and maybe as many as sixty."

"How are the missiles being transported?" Manning asked.

"On a truck," Schuller replied. "Long and flat. Missiles are inside big pipes."

"Pipes?" Hahn raised his eyebrow. "Sewer pipes? *Rohre fur die Kanalanage?*"

"*Ja,*" Schuller confirmed. "*Das ist richtig.*"

"At least it shouldn't be easy to miss," Katz commented. "It'd be nice if something about this mission were easy. Let's head for Prague and hope we get there before Briggs does."

19

Prague is possibly the most magnificent city in Eastern Europe. It is rich in history and culture. Its castles, palaces and cathedrals are breathtaking examples of Gothic, Renaissance and Baroque architecture. Prague has stood for ten centuries and has survived the turbulence of conquest, political conflict and international intrigue.

Yet Prague is more than a relic of the past. It is the seat of the national government and the center of transportation. Modern buildings have appeared among the structures of the past: hospitals, restaurants, clothing stores and even supermarkets. Housing complexes are being built on the outskirts of Prague, ensuring that the historical buildings that dominate the center of the city are not demolished to make way for apartments.

Nove Mesto, the New Town district, is known for its museums, although it is the most modern part of the inner city. Such twentieth-century additions as the main post office and tourist information center are found in Nove Mesto. Railroad tracks bisect Hybernska Street and extend to the main station.

The milk truck containing Phoenix Force slowly drove up Sokolska Mezibranska, passing a row of shops and stores. None of the establishments was open at 6:00 A.M. The streets were deserted. No other vehicles moved. No pedestrians stirred.

"Is it always so quiet at this time in the morning?" Gary Manning asked Cernak from the back of the van.

"I don't know," the Czech replied. "I don't spend much time in Prague and I've never been out on the streets at this hour."

"I have," Karl Hahn declared. "There are usually a few people on the streets. Newspaper trucks and certain vehicles delivering fresh food are generally making stops at this time. Something's wrong, my friends."

"We're almost at the station," Cernak announced as he steered the van onto Vitezneho. The vehicle passed the National Museum on the corner. "If you fellows want to change your plans, let me know now."

"We're being observed," Katz declared. The Israeli peered through the tinted glass of a side window. "There's a man posted on the roof of the museum. I saw sunlight flash against the lens of his binoculars."

"Spotted one on this side, too," Calvin James added as he looked through another window. "There's a dude hiding in an alley. Looks like he's got a two-way radio."

"If we keep going they might simply blast us with a grenade launcher," Manning warned, taking a Remington shotgun from his canvas bag. The Canadian unfolded the SWAT-style metal stock and locked it in place. "Of course, they might blow us away if we try to leave."

"Thanks for making the decision so easy," David McCarter said dryly as he slid the long strap of his Ingram M-10 onto his shoulder and groped inside his bag for some grenades.

"We might as well keep moving forward," Katz told his companions. "We came here to find the terrorists. Maybe we have."

"Maybe they found us, too," James remarked as he finished assembling an M-16. The black warrior attached an

M-203 under the barrel and tightened the sleeve to hold the grenade launcher in place.

"You fucking guys promised me I wouldn't get killed," Cernak complained, but he continued to drive the van toward the main railroad station.

"We're not dead yet," Karl Hahn announced, shoving a banana magazine into the well of his Heckler & Koch MP-5 machine pistol.

"True," Katz agreed, bracing his Uzi submachine gun across the trihook prosthesis attached to the stump of his right arm. The Israeli worked the cocking handle to chamber the first 9 mm parabellum from a 25-round magazine. "And if we get hit by a grenade or rocket, we'll die in less than a second, anyway."

"How comforting," Cernak muttered as the train station appeared straight ahead.

The station was a large modern structure, not unlike what one might find in West Germany or France. The national flag of Czechoslovakia waved gently in the early morning breeze.

Suddenly four uniformed figures appeared from alleys on each side of the street. The soldiers were armed with Model 58 assault rifles, Skorpion machine pistols and one Model 24 submachine gun, which is a 7.62 mm blowback-operated weapon that is a cross between an Israeli Uzi and the old Nazi MP-40 Schmeisser.

Many American firearm experts turn their noses up at a 7.62 mm subgun. These so-called authorities tend to forget that the 7.62 mm is a NATO cartridge used with many of the most respected assault rifles in the world. Some of these same experts have fired Czech-made ammunition and complained that it was of inferior quality and terribly inaccurate. Invariably they fired the heavy-loaded Czech military ammo in gas-operated weapons instead of the blowback subguns designed to handle the hefty loads. The M-24 is a formidable weapon with a muzzle velocity of 1800 fps.

More armed soldiers appeared on the rooftops of buildings. At least one man had a Soviet-made rocket launcher. Half a dozen Czech troops had materialized behind the milk van, covering the vehicle from the rear.

"This situation is becoming terribly unpleasant," Karl Hahn remarked. The German agent sounded far calmer than he felt.

A voice bellowed from a megaphone, shouting orders in Czechoslovakian. Only Hahn and Alexei Cernak understood the message, but an English translation immediately followed.

"This is the State Security and Intelligence Service of the Republic of Czechoslovakia," the voice of Major Ladislav Svoboda declared. "You are ordered to stop your vehicle and surrender immediately. You will step from the van with your hands held at shoulder level. Refuse to obey and I will be forced to tell Major Smetana to order his men to destroy you."

"How did I get in this mess?" Cernak muttered as he stomped on the brake. "This is all your fault, Hahn. I should never have let you talk me into—"

"Get back there," McCarter said gruffly, pulling the big Czech's arm to yank him from his seat. "I'm taking the wheel, mate."

Cernak was seized from behind and hauled into the back of the milk truck. Calvin James shoved him aside and hurried up front with McCarter. Cernak fell into a corner. He glared at Karl Hahn, but the German ignored him. Hahn and Katz were stationed by the side windows. Manning knelt at the rear door. The Canadian had wired together two canister-style grenades. He took a block of white puttylike material from his sack and tore off a small chunk. Manning pushed the piece of C-4 plastic explosive into the gap between the grenades and then inserted a small pencil detonator.

"I'm ready!" Manning announced, reaching for the handle.

"Me, too," McCarter stated as he sat behind the steering wheel.

"Get your head down, man," James told the Briton as he started to raise his M-16. "Time to rock 'n' roll."

McCarter ducked low and covered his head. James squeezed the trigger of the M-203 attached to the rifle barrel. The grenade launcher forced the M-16 back against the black man's hip. A 40 mm projectile burst from the muzzle and smashed through the windshield with ease. The grenade hurtled into the group of soldiers in front of the milk truck.

The high-explosive charge of the grenade went off with monstrous force. The blast tore the soldiers apart and tossed their severed limbs in all directions. McCarter had already pushed his foot to the floor on the gas pedal. The milk truck bolted forward before the dust and mangled body parts could settle.

Manning turned the handle to the rear door, popping it open just enough to toss the two wired grenades outside. The canisters hit the pavement as a volley of automatic fire snarled. Bullets raked the rear of the truck. A slug pierced the metal door less than an inch from the Canadian's face. Manning felt the hot missile sizzle past the tip of his nose as he hastily yanked the door shut.

The C-4 charge exploded, detonating the canisters. The blast was enough to knock down the Czech troops at the rear of the truck. Columns of thick green smoke instantly billowed from the grenades. A dense cloud filled the street as soldiers opened fire with an assortment of weapons.

Bullets ricocheted off the metal body of the van. McCarter turned the wheel sharply to the left. The truck swung onto Ruzova Street. Metal grated when the vehicle scraped against a streetlamp. Tires bounced along the curb as McCarter fought the wheel to keep the van from going totally out of control.

A violent explosion rocked the milk truck. The men in the back of the vehicle were tossed from wall to wall. Katz and Cernak collided. The Czech raised his head sharply, rapping the top of his skull under Yakov's jaw. Katz groaned as pain traveled up his facial nerve. The Israeli's ears rang as he shook his head to clear it.

"I think somebody fired a recoiless rifle at us, or maybe it was a grenade," Manning announced in a loud voice. He assumed that everyone else's ears were ringing as badly as his own. "Whatever it was, it sure went boom."

"By God," McCarter snorted. "You really are an explosives expert. Does it take much time to learn fancy technical jargon like that?"

"Will you just drive?" James urged, poking the barrel of his M-16 through the hole in the windshield. "This mother fucker isn't a tank, man. One well-placed grenade and we go boom-boom to the next world."

"Don't fret so—" McCarter replied, but his sentence ended abruptly. An armored car had rolled into the intersection at Opletalova Street, blocking their escape.

The vehicle was a CZT-70, one of the most advanced armored cars produced in an Eastern-bloc nation. The war machine was equipped with a mounted M-59 light machine gun. The Model 59 resembles the American M-60 and it has a reputation for being as deadly as its Western counterpart. The CZT-79 had too much firepower to try to fight and ramming the armor-plated rhino would be suicidal.

"We've got company coming up from behind!" Manning warned, watching two army jeeps close in fast from the rear.

Calvin James noticed at least one soldier was using the armored car for cover. He triggered the M-16, firing a quick 3-round burst just to convince the trooper to stay down. The 5.56 mm projectiles sang against the steel-plated vehicle, barely scratching the surface.

"Don't do that," Hahn advised. "You might get them mad."

"I think they're already mad, man," James replied, shaking his head. "And we ain't all that sane, or we wouldn't be doing this for a living."

McCarter swung the milk truck into the mouth of an alley between a coffee shop and a leather-goods store. The van smashed into some trash cans, scattering containers and contents as it plunged through the narrow space.

The machine gunner stationed by the Model 59 fired his weapon a second too late. His blast of high velocity 7.62 mm rounds completely missed the milk truck, but one of his own army jeeps swerved right into the salvo. Bullets shattered the windshield and chopped into the chest and face of the driver. The jeep swung out of control and onto the sidewalk.

It rolled forward and nosedived into the large front window of the Konsky Povoz coffee house. Glass exploded as the jeep crashed through the flimsy barrier. It slammed against chairs and tables, ruthlessly rearranging the furniture.

The milk truck continued through the alley. McCarter's eyes widened with surprise and terror when he saw the two-meter-high wooden fence at the end of the alley. He did not know if the van was sturdy enough to crash the fence or what might be on the other side. Of course, he knew what was waiting for them in the street.

McCarter drove the van straight ahead. The front fender struck the barrier forcibly. Wood snapped. Segments of the fence broke off near the base. The hood smashed panels aside. The truck burst through the barrier and collided with the flimsy framework of a large chicken coop. Thin wood snapped and wire popped. Chickens squawked and flapped their wings as they hurried in every direction to avoid the truck.

Feathers covered the windshield. Brown and white figures fluttered around the milk truck as it continued to plunge through the coop. The van struck a post and another wall of the coop caved in. Chickens squawked in panic. McCarter knew from the scratching of talons on metal that at least a couple of birds had managed to get onto the roof of the van. McCarter did not see the fence until a split second before the truck hit it.

Wood gave way to the brute force of the charging vehicle. The fence burst apart and the milk truck rolled into another alley. McCarter turned the wheel to the left and drove the vehicle to the entrance of the alley. He turned right on Opletova. The Czech troops by the armored car saw their quarry bolt onto the deserted street. They shouted at the CZT-79 driver to pursue the truck.

McCarter steered the van onto Jeruzalmeska. An old man, seated on the driver's bench of a small horse-drawn fruit wagon, stared at the van in astonishment. The horse reared with alarm as the milk truck bolted past the wagon. The van traveled the length of Jeruzalmeska without being confronted by any Czech soldiers.

"Maybe we've gotten clear of 'em," Calvin James remarked, but he inserted another cartridge grenade into the breech of the M-203 just in case.

"What the hell is going on?" Karl Hahn wondered aloud. "There were suppose to be terrorists at the railroad station, not Czech soldiers and the STB."

"Schuller and Baker set us up," Cernak decided as he sat breathless on the floor of the van. "They must be working for the STB."

"I don't think so," Katz replied, rubbing his bruised jaw. "More likely someone contacted the STB and told them Briggs and his men were coming to the railroad station. Don't forget, the STB and KGB have been hunting terrorists, too."

"But who tipped them off?" James asked. "Another defector from Briggs's camp?"

"Maybe," the Israeli answered. "Or maybe it was Briggs himself."

"What do you mean?" Cernak asked. "Why would he warn them?"

"Why did he tell his men that the train station would be the site for setting up the missiles?" Katz said with a shrug. "Briggs hadn't shared that information with them before. All he needed to do was tell his drivers where to go. I think he lied about the location just to test his men, just in case some of them went AWOL and told the authorities."

"Which would lead them to the wrong place," Hahn remarked. "Briggs may have felt this would be an advantage. Divert the authorities to one place while the real action is taking place in another part of the city."

"But where?" Cernak inquired.

"Better figure that out later," Manning advised. "We're not off the STB hit parade yet."

As if to confirm the Canadian's warning, an army jeep swung onto Jindrisska Street. The troopers had mounted a Model 59 machine gun on the vehicle. They opened fire with the blaster. A column of 7.62 mm rounds struck the broadside of the milk truck. Bullets pierced the side of the van. Alexei Cernak screamed and sprawled on his side. Blood splurted from two bullet wounds in his left side. A stray slug ricocheted off a rivet inside the van. The bullet bounced and landed in Karl Hahn's lap. He glanced down at the misshapen lump of lead. His hand trembled as he brushed the slug aside.

McCarter rapidly steered the milk truck onto Senova Zna. The jeep followed, quickly closing in on its target. The military vehicle was faster than the van, and the soldiers' M-59 had far greater range than the subguns carried by most of the men of Phoenix Force. Another salvo of 7.62 mm slugs raked the milk truck. The vehicle jerked to one side. Two bullets had struck a rear tire. McCarter would not let a flat slow them down; he was prepared to drive the truck on four hubs if he had to.

"Alexei's been hit!" Katz shouted.

Calvin James darted to the back of the van. Hahn shuffled up front to ride shotgun for McCarter. James knelt by the bloodied figure of Alexei Cernak. The Phoenix Force medic shook his head. Their Czech friend's wound was bad. Maybe too bad.

"Is that launcher loaded?" Manning asked as he crouched by the rear door. "Be my guest. I'm busy, anyway."

Manning opened the door and swung the M-16 at the Czech army jeep. The soldiers were having difficulty handling the machine gun while the Jeep sped after the fleeing van. Manning snap-aimed the '16 and triggered the M-203 attachment. A 40 mm grenade rocketed from the muzzle and crashed into the jeep. The powerful projectile exploded, blasting the military vehicle into a collection of mangled metal and shredded flesh. The gasoline ignited spraying flames across the grisly wreckage.

"Christ," the Canadian muttered with disgust as he yanked the door shut. "We're killing a bunch of guys who think we're the same bunch of terrorists we're after. Those poor bastards are just doing their job, same as us."

"If you think of a way we can sit down and talk with the STB and the KGB without winding up in front of a firing squad, let me know," Katz said sharply. "Survival is the name of the game, and in this case there are more lives at stake than our own.''

"How's Alexei?'' Karl Hahn asked, glancing over his shoulder at the wounded Czech.

"Not good,'' James said grimly as he plunged a syringe into Cernak's arm and injected a dose of morphine. "Looks like he caught a bullet in a kidney. Maybe in his liver, too.''

"Can you do anything for him?'' Katz inquired.

"Sure,'' James replied, reaching into his medic kit. "I can give him enough morphine to let him die without pain.''

20

The Lanterna Magika was a very popular restaurant strategically located between the Wallenstein Palace and St. Nicholas's Church. It specialized in fine Bohemian food, the best Russian vodka and delightful French wines. Yet its greatest attraction was probably the view. In addition to the Wallenstein Palace and St. Nicholas's, it offered an excellent view of St. Vitus's Cathedral and the Royal Summer House. From the second-story picture window, one could see the National Gallery and, of course, Prague Castle.

The restaurant usually opened at 11:30 A.M. However, the place was already crowded at nine o'clock that morning. The front door had been forced with a crowbar. Tables and chairs had been moved from the dining hall and placed against windows. Men armed with an assortment of American- and German-made weapons had moved into position.

The flatbed truck was parked in front of the Lanterna Magika. Men dressed in overalls and caps carried long cylinder-shaped objects that looked like rolled-up carpets into the restaurant. Four men carried a large wooden crate from the truck, each holding an end of the steel rods that ran through metal rings on the sides of the container.

They were breathing hard when they entered the Lanterna Magika. The crate was heavy and all four men were filled with tension, well aware of what the box contained. Colonel Zackery Briggs and Herman Drache approached the crate.

"Are you certain that thing will protect us from the plu tonium?" Drache asked, obviously nervous about being in the same room with the deadly radioactive material.

"Captain Heywood assured me it would be safe," Briggs replied. "In fact, the Captain said that it won't even be ne cessary to remove the plutonium from the lead container that are inside the crate. Each canister needs only to b placed into the warhead of a missile. The warheads will ex plode on impact and ignite the detonators. Beautiful in it simplicity, isn't it?"

"I wouldn't wish to disagree with you, Colonel," Drach said dryly. "Maybe we should get four other men to hau that thing upstairs. These fellows look pretty tired."

"Yes," Briggs said with a nod. "We don't want anyon dropping the plutonium. At least not unless it's to blow th hell out of some damned Commies."

"I'm hoping that won't be necessary," the German ad mitted.

"That's all in the hands of God, my friend," the Ameri can remarked, his eyes gazing at a wall as if peering a something only he could see. "Are you familiar with th Bible, Drache? Do you recall the sixth chapter of the Bool of Revelations?"

"Not offhand, sir," Drache confessed.

"It describes the Four Horsemen of the Apocalypse," Briggs explained. "It is believed they symbolize famine disease, war and death. With these will be the beginning o the end of the world. We may very well be in the last days Have you thought about that?"

"No more than I have to," Drache muttered.

"Look at the famine in Ethiopia and other parts of Af rica," Briggs continued, barely noticing Drache's remark "Then there is the modern pestilence of AIDS. That leave two Horsemen," the colonel declared. "The rider on the re horse, who is War, and the last rider. 'Behold a pale horse

and he who sat on him was Death.' Perhaps we are the final
Horsemen of the Apocalypse. It may be God's will that we
pave the way for Armageddon."

"I . . . I hope you haven't mentioned this to the men,"
Drache began awkwardly. "It might make them a bit nervous."

"Of course not," Briggs assured him. "They're good
soldiers, but they aren't men of vision. They would fail to
understand that it doesn't matter how things go this day. We
will win whether the Communists free Czechoslovakia or we
are forced to launch the missiles."

"That's . . . very reassuring, sir," Drache told him.

"I'm going upstairs to take charge of setting up the missiles and making certain we've got the field radio on the
right frequencies to contact the Soviet Embassy and the
Commie slime at the castle. You're in charge of the downstairs operation. Make sure the men are ready. Everyone
should have weapons, ammunition and M-17 protective
masks."

"That is confusing, sir," Drache started. "If the Czech
military is ordered to attack us, you said you'd launch the
missiles. Yet you insisted we bring gas masks."

"That's just in case the local police take an interest in us
before we've had time to set up the missiles and contact the
Reds. After all, we've obviously broken into this restaurant. We've even barricaded the windows. Someone is
bound to notice and call the cops. They might manage to lob
some tear gas into the building before our men can pick
them off."

"Colonel Briggs," interrupted Corporal Plinicek, a
Czech-American WAFN member who was assigned to
communications due to his fluency in Czechoslovakian.
"Are you certain none of our people went to the main railroad station in Nove Mesto by mistake?"

"Positive," Briggs replied, a trace of irritation in his tone. "That story was simply false information to prevent possible traitors within our camp from betraying us. I also contacted the local police and told them there would be an attack on the station. Thought that might keep them busy while we moved into position here."

"They've been busy all right," Plinicek stated. "So is the Czech army, and probably the STB. According to a radio report, there was a gun battle in the Nove Mesto section. They say a gang of terrorists clashed with soldiers about two hours ago. Some of the gang is still at large. They're to be regarded as armed and extremely dangerous. They killed a number of soldiers, but the state radio station isn't saying how many bought the farm. Apparently they've initiated an intensive manhunt all over Prague for those guys."

"Was ist das?" Drache wondered aloud. "What the hell is going on, Colonel?"

"I don't know," Briggs said with a frown. "Probably some sort of trick by the Commies."

"What would they have to gain?" Drache asked.

"The only thing I can think of is that Schuller and Baker might have tried some sort of foolhardy stunt and triggered the gun battle," the colonel said with a shrug.

"Schuller and Baker?" Drache shook his head. "I can't imagine those two cowards trying something like that. Besides, neither of them is an especially skilled fighter. On top of that, they ran out on us...."

"Look," Briggs began with a sigh. "I don't have an answer to this and I really don't care. The matter doesn't concern us unless this manhunt leads the police here. Of course, it means we'll have to act quickly. If the soldiers are involved in the dragnet, they could force us to launch the missiles before we've had a chance to contact the Reds."

"We're running out of time," Drache said grimly. "One way or the other."

MAJOR LADISLAV SVOBODA EXAMINED the bullet-ridden wreck that had formerly been the milk truck. The vehicle had been abandoned behind a scrap-metal bin at a tool factory in Old Town. The STB agent peered inside. The walls of the van had been punctured by several bullets, but not by as many as Svoboda had hoped.

"Where's the body?" he asked a young lieutenant in the Czechoslovakian infantry. The junior officer's search team had discovered the van.

"Over here, sir," the lieutenant answered, gesturing at the still form covered by an army blanket. "The man was dead when we got here. His companions had folded up a jacket and placed it under his head. I think they tried to make his dying as easy as possible. We found four plastic syringes beside the corpse."

"Four?" Svoboda raised his eyebrows. "Any idea what the syringes might have contained?"

"There hasn't been a lab test done and I am no chemist...."

"I ask your opinion as a soldier," Svoboda explained as he knelt by the corpse and pulled back the blanket. Alexei Cernak's face seemed very peaceful. His expression was almost pleasant.

"A medic might carry penicillin, morphine or codeine, perhaps."

"I don't think this man bled to death," Svoboda remarked. "But his wounds would have killed him. I suspect they gave him an overdose of morphine. He was probably floating up to the moon when he died."

"Not a bad way to go, sir" the lieutenant commented.

The roar of thunder startled Svoboda. He glanced up at the black clouds that seemed to have suddenly blotted out the sun. He had not noticed that the sky was getting dark. Rain pelted his face. Svoboda turned to the lieutenant.

"Did you find anything to suggest where the other terrorists went or how many men we're looking for?" he asked.

"The surface is covered with gravel, sir," the young officer pointed out. "Doesn't make for very good tracks. Workers have trampled the area and I don't know how to tell one indentation of gravel from another."

"The rain won't help, either," the STB officer commented.

"Sir," the army lieutenant began. "Isn't there any news about the other terrorists?"

"What other terrorists?" Svoboda asked. "The men from the van are the only ones we're looking for."

"But surely they had other accomplices," the lieutenant remarked. "I heard that fourteen soldiers were killed during the gun battle in New Town."

"Sixteen soldiers were killed and a few others were wounded," the STB man admitted. "But the men from this truck didn't have any accomplices. They managed quite well on their own."

"They're even more dangerous than we were led to believe," the young officer commented, a trace of alarm in his voice. He turned up his collar to keep the rain from running down his neck. "Is it true they're Americans? I thought Americans were supposed to be decadent and weak."

"All we know for sure is that they're a serious threat," Svoboda told him. "They have to be found and found quickly."

"Sir," the lieutenant began. "There's a rumor that these men have plutonium stolen from a train accident...."

"Don't put too much stock in rumors, Lieutenant," the STB agent urged. "But we can't dismiss any possibility at this time."

"Yes, sir," the lieutenant said, nodding.

"You've done a good job," Svoboda told him with a weak smile. "I'll make certain you receive the recognition you deserve."

"*Mockrat dekuji,*" the young officer replied.

Major Svoboda nodded in reply. He wondered if anyone would ever thank him for anything again. Captain Renkov of the KGB certainly would not thank him if the terrorists escaped. The Tatar would certainly use Svoboda as a scapegoat to try to protect himself from the anger of the Kremlin.

The rain continued to pound Svoboda. The cold sank into his flesh. Cold and clammy as death.

21

The blue Klenot cruised the streets of Mala Strana. The car was a large four-door similar to an American Cadillac. Calvin James had no trouble hot-wiring the Klenot, although he had reluctantly agreed to let Karl Hahn drive. Yakov Katzenelenbogen sat in the passenger seat next to Hahn and the other three members of Phoenix Force were crammed into the back. Their weapons were hidden on the floor as the German agent drove the car up Pod Bruskou.

"If we don't find something pretty soon the cops are gonna find us," Calvin James warned. "They've probably found the milk truck by now and figure we're either hiding somewhere or that we've got another set of wheels. When the owner of this jalopy reports this car stolen..."

"The terrorists must be in this area," Karl Hahn declared. "They'll want to get as close to Prague Castle and the Soviet Embassy as possible to make certain the missiles are on target."

"But what if they're not doing it today?" David McCarter commented, chewing on the end of an unlit Player's cigarette. "Briggs lied to his troops about the location of the missiles. He might have lied about when detonation would take place, as well."

"I doubt it," Katz replied. "If Briggs suspected that some of his people might go AWOL, he wouldn't hang around the base and risk an attack. The terrorists will make their move today. In fact, they're probably already in position now."

"And the only hope we have of finding them is if we can locate the flatbed with sewer pipes," Gary Manning said with a sigh. "That's a hell of a long shot."

"But it's all we've got to work on," Hahn stated as he drove the Klenot onto Letenska.

They passed the magnificent Wallenstein Palace. The ornate statues and fountains of the palace are classic examples of the Czech Baroque art period. The palace is also noted for its beautiful flower gardens. However, Phoenix Force was not on a sight-seeing tour. They barely glanced at the Wallenstein Palace as they continued to search for the terrorists.

"Look at that," Katz announced, gesturing with the steel hooks of his prosthesis. The Israeli pointed at a large flatbed truck parked at the curb, roughly two blocks ahead. "We may have found our quarry."

"Looks as though it's parked in front of the Lanterna Magika—the Magic Lantern," Hahn said. "A high-class restaurant. Popular with well-to-do tourists, Czech politicians and foreign diplomats from the embassies along Triziste and Thunovska."

"Including the Soviet Embassy," Manning commented.

"The Magic Lantern sounds familiar," Katz remarked. "Isn't that what the Czechs call a type of stage performance that combines live actors and dancers with performers projected on a screen?"

"It's a very popular art form in Czechoslovakia," Hahn confirmed. "The Czechs have always been lovers of music, dance and other fine arts. Cinema is very popular here, too. A number of Czech films have won Academy Awards."

"Well, that's bloody fascinating," McCarter said sharply, rolling his eyes with annoyance. "But we've got a job to do...."

"Don't worry," Hahn replied as he steered the car into the mouth of an alley. "But we can't just drive up to the Lanterna Magika and knock on the door."

"They've certainly got sentries posted," Manning stated. "Lookouts are probably watching the streets like a bunch of hungry hawks. Any vehicle that appears remotely suspicious will probably get blown to bits if it gets too close."

"So will anybody who approaches on foot," James remarked. "Anybody bring along an invisibility cloak?"

"Maybe we won't need one," Hahn commented, listening to the tap-tap of raindrops striking the roof of the Klenot. The rain came down harder and faster. The rattle sounded vaguely like pellets fired from a full-auto BB gun.

"The rain will reduce visibility," Gary Manning said with a nod. "But not enough to be sure we'll reach the restaurant alive."

The roar of thunder bellowed like the groan of a giant sky god. The darkness of the thunderclouds had turned midmorning into midnight. A flash of lightning illuminated the streets for an instant. Thunder followed with a rumble not unlike cannon fire.

"It's not a sure thing," Katz agreed. "But it's the only thing in our favor. We don't have time to put together a complicated strategy. The thunderstorm is offering us some natural camouflage. Let's take advantage of it."

"Damn right," the eager-for-action McCarter said as he gathered up his Ingram M-10. "This rain is sort of an act of God. Shouldn't turn your nose up at a gift from the heavens."

"Who can argue with that?" Calvin James said with a shrug. He reached for his M-16. "Let's go kick some ass."

The five men emerged from the car. Heavy rain pelted them. They tugged on their hats and caps to shield their eyes and turned up their collars to keep the rain off their necks. Each man opened his coat or windbreaker and held his weapon inside the garment, using it to partially conceal the firearm and to prevent the firing mechanism from getting soaked. They did not mind this inconvenience. The heavier the rainfall, the better camouflage it would provide.

"Wait for the lightning," Hahn advised as he led the way to the mouth of the alley. "The streets will be lit up for a split second, followed by pitch darkness and thunder. The effect will be like a flashbulb in a dark room. It'll be difficult for the enemy to see us and the thunder should cover any noise we make."

"Nice theory," Manning commented. "Let's see if it works."

Lightning flashed. Phoenix Force waited a moment for the darkness to return. The men darted forward as thunder growled from the sky. The fighting unit jogged to the corner of a wall that surrounded a library. They flattened their backs against the wall, melting into the shadows.

"You know those blokes might have infrared," McCarter whispered. Rain had soaked through the Briton's wool hat. He tried to shake water from his face as he blinked to keep his vision clear.

"I doubt they brought infrared for a mission in the middle of the morning," Manning replied. "Besides, they wouldn't use night scanners during a thunderstorm. First flash of lightning that occurred would almost boil your eyeballs if you saw it through infrared lenses."

"There's an alley between the Lanterna Magika and a novelty shop up ahead," Hahn explained. "The dining-room windows and a side door to the kitchen of the restaurant open onto the alley."

"It's probably occupied, gentlemen," Katz warned. "I've got a silencer on my Uzi. David, you've got a muffler on your Ingram, don't you?"

"Yeah," the Briton replied. "How about you, Gary?"

"A silencer on a shotgun?" Manning snorted. "Cute, David. Actually, there is a type of silenced shotgun shell, but I'm afraid I don't have any with me."

"Didn't put a suppressor on my '16, either," James added. "But there's a silencer on my Commander."

Another fork of lightning filled the sky. Phoenix Force used the same tactic as before. They waited for darkness and scrambled to the novelty shop as thunder boomed. Hahn, McCarter and James wedged into the narrow doorway of the shop. Katz crouched behind a trash can by the curb. Manning had to use the skimpy cover of a lamppost. Water soaked through his pant leg as he turned sideways, trying to make the most of the shelter.

"One more time," Manning whispered, eager to move to a less vulnerable position.

As if on cue, the lightning flashed once more. Phoenix Force broke cover when darkness returned. The thunder did not seem as loud as the splash of boots striking mud puddles as they dashed to the alley. The hammering of their hearts seemed to drown out the sound of thunder. Yet no enemy shots were fired.

McCarter reached the objective first. He poked the silencer-equipped muzzle of his Ingram around the corner as he peered into the alley. Three men were seated on small wooden crates, huddled under the shelter of a canvas tarp that had become an improvised lean-to. An odd-looking weapon was mounted on a bipod between two of the men. At first glance McCarter thought the gun resembled a giant British Sten. It was, in fact, a Czech ZK-383 submachine gun. A powerful 9 mm weapon, the ZK-383 has an accelerated cyclic rate of 700 rpm if the block is removed from the bolt. One hell of an alley cleaner.

The British commando did not hesitate. He was armed with an impressive blaster, as well. His compact M-10 had an even greater rate of fire than the ZK-383, although the stubby barrel could not match the range of accuracy of the Czech chatterbox. At close quarters the latter was of little importance.

McCarter opened fire. Parabellum slugs coughed from the muzzle of the silencer. The men in the alley screamed as bullets tore into flesh. One man reached for the ZK-383. He bent over to receive a 9 mm messenger through the forehead. One of his comrades was doubled up, trying to keep his intestines from seeping out of the trio of bullet holes in his gut. McCarter hit him with another burst of Ingram rounds, chopping the guy's heart into pulp.

The third opponent had thrown himself clear of the lean-to a split second before McCarter opened fire. A WAFN lunatic, he carried a Government Colt in a GI regulation button-flap holster on his hip. The American terrorist realized he could not open the holster and draw the weapon in time to get the drop on McCarter. It required less time simply to lunge at the British warrior.

McCarter only needed one full second to take out the two terrorists by the ZK-383 chattergun, but that was enough time for the WAFN fanatic to make his move. The Briton turned as his third opponent leaped forward. Hands grabbed the M-10 and shoved it upward to point the barrel at the sky. The Yankee Doodle dimwit tried to ram a knee into McCarter's crotch, but the Phoenix fighter shifted a leg and blocked the kick with his thigh.

The Briton turned sharply and pushed his attacker into the brick wall of the Lanterna Magika. McCarter's head shot forward, butting the hard front of his skull into the bridge of his opponent's nose. The British warrior butted the terrorist again. The head butt drove the man's skull backward to painfully connect with the wall. McCarter snapped his arms forward and punted the steel frame of his Ingram into the American's jaw.

"Need a hand?" Manning whispered as he joined the Briton in the alley.

"No thanks, mate," McCarter replied as he slammed a solid left hook to his opponent's temple.

The man fell to the ground at McCarter's feet. The British ace kicked him behind the ear to make certain the fellow did not wake up for a while. The other members of Phoenix Force had entered the alley. Katz covered the side door with his Uzi while Hahn and James trained their weapons on the mouth of the alley. Manning pointed his Remington shotgun at a second-story window. McCarter drew a strip of unbreakable plastic from his belt. He used the riot cuffs to bind the unconscious man's wrists together at the small of his back.

"Did you know there's a guy out there in that fuckin' truck?" Calvin James rasped. "He's been sitting in the cab of that flatbed all along."

"Bastard must be deaf," McCarter said with a shrug. "Those blokes let out quite a yell when I burned them."

"The rain makes a lot of noise, thank God," Katz remarked. "The fellow in the truck might also have a radio playing."

"He's bound to see us when we move to the front of the building," Manning warned.

"We'll take care of him, then," the Phoenix Force commander replied. "The missiles are our most important concern. Karl, you said there's a skylight to the Magic Lantern."

"That's right," Hahn confirmed. "They'll almost certainly launch the missiles through the skylight from the second story."

"And you said they wouldn't have a sentry on the roof," McCarter commented as he slipped off his soaking-wet jacket to remove a coil of rope from his right shoulder.

"The roof is slanted and there's no place to stand unless they have somebody squatting on the peak like a chimpanzee," the German explained. "Maybe if the weather were better, but with this rain a sentry would likely slip off the roof and break his neck."

"All right," Katz began. "Everybody knows what to do. Just remember who and what we're dealing with. Don't take any chances with these lunatics. Kill everybody in the building if you have to, but don't let them launch those damn missiles."

James also removed his jacket and took a coil of rope from his shoulder. Hahn slipped a canvas sack from his back and removed two grappling hooks that had folding blades. He locked the hooks in place. James and McCarter hastily knotted the ropes to the hooks while Gary Manning fitted a C-4 charge just above the knob of the side door. The Canadian demolitions expert inserted a radio-operated detonator with a special blasting cap into the plastique. Manning nodded in self-approval.

McCarter cautiously moved to the end of the alley, his Ingram in one fist and the grapnel in the other. Calvin James shouldered his M-16 and drew his silenced .45 Colt. Hahn carried the other hook and rope as well as his Heckler & Koch MP-5.

"Hey!" a voice called from the rear of the building. "Did one of you guys yell for somethin'?"

McCarter was startled by the voice, but the man's remarks suggested he had not heard the cries of his comrades clearly enough to know that they had screamed in pain. Probably a guard assigned to patrol outside, McCarter decided.

"Look," the voice continued. "Do you fuckers want somethin' or not? I'm not your damn servant, man."

"Hold on," the Briton replied, mimicking a Midwest American accent. "I'll come to you."

McCarter stepped around the corner. He held the Ingram high, canted on a shoulder, pointing toward the cloudy sky. The Briton held the grappling hook in clear view as he approached a figure wearing a yellow slicker with matching hood. The WAFN flunky did not appear to carry a weapon, but McCarter assumed the guy had a pistol under his coat. The terrorist strained his eyes, probably trying to recognize the man who had answered his question.

"Did anybody tell you what the hell we're supposed to do with this thing?" McCarter inquired, gently swinging the grappling hook at the end of his rope.

"What is it?" the WAFN goon questioned as he stared through the stormy darkness. "A hook?"

"Oh, yeah," the Briton confirmed. Rain splashed his face as he glanced up at a balcony on the second floor. He noticed that all the first-story windows were boarded up. Apparently Briggs's people were more worried about protecting themselves from a standard police raid than maintaining visual contact with the outside.

"Shit," the sentry said with a shrug. "I don't know what we're supposed to do with it. Who gave you that thing?"

"The Colonel," McCarter answered.

"And he didn't—" The terrorist stopped suddenly as a flash of lightning illuminated the Briton's face. "I've never seen you before—"

McCarter's arm snapped forward, lashing the rope and hook across the guard's shoulder and neck. The terrorist groaned as the prongs caught at the shoulder blades. The British ace yanked the rope hard and pulled the terrorist forward. He swung his booted foot, kicking the man squarely between the legs. The sentry uttered a high-pitched wheezing sound. McCarter backhanded the frame of his Ingram across the man's jaw. The guard fell to one knee.

"Silly sod," the Briton rasped as he chopped the side of his hand across the base of his opponent's neck. The man fell on his face as easily as a statue tipped from its pedestal.

James glanced down at the motionless sentry as McCarter estimated the distance to the roof. The Briton swung his hook by its rope, increasing the centrifugal force until he was ready for the throw.

"Did you kill this guy, Dave?" James inquired as he also got his hook and rope ready.

"I'm not sure," McCarter replied. "He's not going anywhere for a while either way."

The black commando simply shrugged and started to spin his grappling hook. Karl Hahn drew a foot-long Interarms silencer from an inside jacket pocket and fitted it to the threaded muzzle of his H&K machine pistol. The rain made the metal slippery. Hahn cursed under his breath as he tried to screw the suppressor into place.

McCarter hurled his grappler. The hook sailed in a high arc and landed on the roof with a loud thump. The Briton pulled the rope sharply. The hook slid down the overhang of the roof and snared on the iron cresting at the cornice.

The Phoenix pro tugged the rope to be certain the hook would hold. He grabbed it and braced his feet against the wall. The surface was damp and the rope was drenched by the rain, but McCarter was the most experienced mountaineer in the five-man army. His boots slipped more than once and his fists slid on the rope. Yet McCarter's skill and stubbornness allowed him to keep moving steadily and quickly upward.

James threw his hook onto the balcony. A tug latched the grappler to the handrail. The black warrior climbed the rope hand over hand, trapping the line with his feet to help keep his grip on the slippery cord. James and McCarter were defenseless as they climbed the ropes, relying on Karl Hahn to cover them from the ground below.

Calvin James's hand gripped the balcony railing. He started to pull himself over the rail when the French windows to the balcony burst open. A German gunman, armed with a Walther MPL submachine gun, charged across the threshold. The sound of the grappling hooks striking the roof and the balcony had not gone unnoticed by the terrorists in the second-story dining hall. The UGNP flunky started to swing his weapon toward James's position.

The three muffled reports from Karl Hahn's silenced MP-5 were barely heard above the howl of the rainstorm. A trio of slugs punctured the center of the neo-Nazi's chest. The impact hurled the UGNP cretin backward through the French windows. Glass shattered when his body collided with a windowpane before falling to the floor.

Voices shouted an assortment of profanities and commands in both German and English. Two circular objects were hurled through the open windows. The grenades sailed over the balcony rail and plunged over the side.

"Scheisser!" Karl Hahn shouted as he bolted to the alley and dived for cover.

The German BND agent landed face down in a mud puddle and wrapped his arms around his head. The grenades exploded in unison. The body of the WAFN sentry, whom McCarter had taken out moments before, was torn to shreds. There was no longer any need to question whether the man was dead.

"This is Colonel Zackery Briggs of the World Army Freedom Network!" a voice bellowed in English through the loudspeakers of an amplifier. "As you are no doubt aware, I am armed with four missiles that have plutonium warheads. They are ready to be fired at Prague Castle, the Soviet Embassy, the House of Nations and the House of the People. If you do not retreat immediately I will launch these missiles, and the consequences will be on your head. You have exactly three minutes to clear the area before I give the command to fire."

22

David McCarter slithered along the roof cresting toward the skylight. He understood why no sentries had been posted on there. The footing was treacherous and the rain had made the situation worse. The Briton inched along the slippery tiles. The iron cresting moved under his weight and the rusty metal threatened to give way at any moment.

The Phoenix Force commando had heard Briggs's warning and he realized that the psychotic colonel was entirely capable of carrying out his claim. A voice boomed from the amplifier in rapid Czechoslovakian, no doubt translating the colonel's demands.

McCarter shuffled to the skylight and peered through the glass. The furniture of the second-story dining room had been pushed to the walls to make room for the missiles. The former SAS sergeant was a superb pilot, but he knew little about missiles, rockets or nuclear weapons. Colonel Briggs's missile system seemed primitive. The rockets were only two yards long and appeared to be made of aluminum and plastic. Only the steel warheads seemed to be sturdy enough to cause any damage.

The missiles were mounted on metal tracks pointing toward the skylight. A radio control panel sat on a small field table. Two men stood by the controls. McCarter had seen only pictures of Zackery Briggs in the newspapers, but he was certain the gray-haired man with the silver eagles pinned to his collar had to be the famous fanatic. The British ace had no idea who the other joker might be. Whoever the guy was, his hands were poised over the control panel as he waited for instructions from Colonel Briggs.

McCarter decided this was enough to earn the fellow a death sentence.

The Briton had not made this decision without weighing other possibilities. None of the men of Phoenix Force was a murderer. McCarter enjoyed action and he thrived on combat, but he found no sadistic pleasure in killing, especially when it was quite in self-defense. However, faced with the choice of killing one sick fanatic—or a hundred sick fanatics—to save the lives of thousands of innocent people, McCarter had no moral conflicts to wrestle with.

He did not hesitate. The Briton drew his Browning Hi-Power from shoulder leather. McCarter chose the pistol because he could trust its accuracy. He snapped off the safety, aimed and fired.

A 115 grain slug punched through the glass skylight. The hot glob of copper and lead sliced into the room and descended like a high-speed bolt of lightning. Captain Heywood uttered a loud moan as the bullet struck his face just under his left eye.

The 9 mm splintered the orbital bone. Heywood's eyeball popped from its socket, swinging from the thick cord of the optic nerve. Blood streamed down his cheek as the captain staggered away from the control panel. McCarter squeezed off two more shots, pumping both parabellums into Heywood's chest. The WAFN officer gasped and vomited crimson. He fell, lifeless, to the floor.

"Damn you to hell!" Colonel Briggs snarled as he swung his Government Colt pistol toward the skylight.

McCarter's weapon snarled again. A fourth bullet shattered glass. Briggs's arm suddenly spun like an airplane propeller. A dizzling hot 9 mm slug tore through his right biceps and snapped bone before drilling a destructive exit at the colonel's triceps. Briggs's .45 pistol seemed to leap from his hand as blood squirted from the severed arteries of his bullet-wrecked arm.

A WAFN bodyguard quickly shoved his commander away from the missile control panel, as it appeared to be the immediate target. Another enforcer raised a Smith & Wesson subgun and triggered a burst of 9 mm rounds at the skylight. McCarter rolled on his back, moving clear of the window. Glass exploded from the skylight as the WAFN gunman tried to strike back at the rooftop marksman.

Calvin James, in position on the balcony, took an orange canister grenade from his belt. He pulled the pin and tossed the grenade low. The canister rolled across the floor as James dashed through the French windows, his M-16 held ready.

The WAFN flunky with the S&W chopper and a German fanatic armed with a Steyr 9 mm subgun—an Austrian version of the Uzi—were busy blasting the hell out of the skylight. They did not notice James until the black man's assault rifle was pointed in their direction. The terrorists tried to train their weapons on James, but they were not quick enough to live.

The M-16 snarled a 3-round burst. A trio of 5.56 mm projectiles hammered through the rib cage of the WAFN gunman. His heart and lungs were ripped apart by the high-velocity slugs. The American terrorist opened his mouth, but he could not scream because blood had already bubbled up into his throat. The WAFN slob fired the last of the S&W subgun's ammo into the ceiling as he fell backward and dropped into death.

James swung his rifle toward the UGNP triggerman. The German's face twisted into an ugly mask of rage when he saw that his opponent was a black man. The stocky UGNP zealot was a Hitler-loving moron who believed in the Aryan "master race." He even wore a replica of the Iron Cross pinned to his left breast pocket. The terrorist felt insulted that a mere *"Schwartzie"* would dare to threaten him.

The UGNP killer raised his Steyr to open fire. James's M-16 nailed him with a 3-round burst before the German could squeeze the trigger. A 5.56 mm hornet struck the phony

Nazi medal on his chest and pierced the center of its swastika. The other two copper-jacketed projectiles ripped open his throat and abruptly dismantled vertebrae in his neck. The neo-Nazi hit the floor in a twitching heap. His convulsions soon stopped forever. Perhaps his soul would finally meet his mentor in hell.

The canister grenade spewed pinkish-gray smoke. The mist was not dense, but the effects were very rapid. The remaining WAFN and UGNP flunkies began to cough violently and clutched their abdomens. Most fumbled with their M-17 projectile masks as they desperately tried to pull the contraptions over their faces.

Corporal Plinicek, the Czech-American WAFN translator, did not waste time with his mask. He braced himself against a wall as his stomach turned and his bladder lost control. Tears filled his eyes and mucus ran from his nostrils. Yet he raised his Uzi subgun and tried to clear his vision enough to aim at Calvin James.

Three 9 mm slugs split Plinicek's face, punching holes in his forehead and nose. The back of his skull exploded, splashing blood and brain matter across the wall. David McCarter watched the dead man slump to the floor. A thread of smoke rose from the muzzle of his silenced Ingram machine pistol.

The Briton pulled the pin from another canister grenade and dropped it through the skylight. More pink-gray mist floated inside the room. The terrorists doubled up in agony. They defecated and urinated in their pants. Vomit rose to their mouths. They were too sick to stand, never mind to fight.

Their M-17 protective masks were useless because the Phoenix Force commandos had used a strong nausea gas mixed with dimethyl sulphoxide. DMSO increases the absorption level of other substances. This allowed the nausea gas to rapidly pass through the pores of the terrorists' skin to the bloodstream. The five men of Phoenix Force had previously taken an antidote, so they were immune to the effects of the nausea mist.

The terrorists rolled on the floor, many of them choking on their own vomit. The masks actually made their condition worse. The devices designed to protect the men were threatening to smother them. One man panicked and stumbled to the French windows, intending to pry his mask off and suck clean air into his agonized lungs. His motor senses were uncoordinated due to the gas. He ran onto the balcony and collided with the handrail. The terrorist tumbled over the railing and plunged to the hard ground fifteen feet below.

Colonel Zackery Briggs slowly rose from the floor, clutching his shattered right arm with his left hand. Through tear-fogged eyes he saw Calvin James approach. Briggs blinked with surprise. What was a black man doing here? There were certainly no blacks in the ranks of the WAFN or the UGNP, and the Czechoslovakians did not have any blacks in their military or police.

"You..." Briggs began, coughing forcibly. "You're a nigger...."

"You're an asshole," James replied.

He suddenly swatted the plastic stock of his M-16 against Briggs's bullet-broken arm. The colonel shrieked in agony and fainted. James calmly stepped over the senseless fanatic to check on the remaining terrorists.

YAKOV KATZENELENBOGEN and Gary Manning had been equally as busy on the first story of the Lanterna Magika. When they heard the hand grenade explode, both men immediately went into action. Katz stepped from the alley as the terrorist in the flatbed truck emerged from the rig with an H&K G-3A-3 assault rifle in his fists. He might as well have been armed with a lollipop. Katz fired the Uzi. The Interarms sound suppressor reduced the report of the Israeli's subgun to a burp-pop, but the 9 mm slugs still found their target and ripped the terrorist from solar plexus to throat.

Manning had already planted C-4 charges at the side door and two windows. He pressed the rubberized button of a remote-control packet to set off the radio detonators inserted in each charge. Three explosions occurred at once. The door and windows were blown apart. Manning and Katz jogged to the ragged holes that had been windows and lobbed gas grenades into the building.

While the restaurant filled with nausea gas, Manning and Katz moved to the alley. The Canadian demolitions expert yanked the pin from a concussion grenade and rolled it to the front door. The Phoenix pair ducked behind shelter as the grenade exploded, blasting the front entrance.

Gary Manning climbed through a shattered window, his Remington shotgun held ready. The dining hall resembled the aftermath of a blitzkrieg bombing. The furniture that had been stacked against the doors and windows had been scattered across the room by the explosions. Several terrorists lay dead, killed by the unexpected blasts. One man's chest had been impaled by a broken chair leg. Many terrorists were vomiting and cringing from the nausea gas. A few had managed to pull on protective masks, unaware that the M-17 gear would not help.

Two UGNP thugs held weapons although they were spitting up mucus and pawing at their eyes. Manning pointed his shotgun at the pair and whistled sharply. Both men turned toward the sound.

"Auf Wiedersehen," the Canadian announced as he triggered the Remington.

A 12-gauge blast of double-O buckshot smashed the closest man's chest into a bloody crushed hull of broken bone splinters and pulped organs. The impact of the multiple pellets hurled the terrorist five feet. His comrade quickly dropped to one knee and swung his MPL subgun toward the Canadian.

Manning fired the shotgun once more. Buckshot slammed into the second terrorist's face. His skull exploded as though it were a blood balloon. The decapitated corpse slumped to the floor, a river of scarlet pumping from the ragged stump of its neck.

Two panic-stricken terrorists bolted for the front door. Katzenelenbogen stepped directly into their path. The Israeli's Uzi burned a trio of parabellum upward into the nearest man's solar plexus. The bullets burned a merciless path into the terrorist's heart and punched three messy exits between his shoulder blades.

The other terrorist was armed with an M-14 rifle. He was too close to Katz to fire the weapon from shoulder or hip, so he slashed the barrel at the Israeli's head. Steel rang against steel. The astonished terrorist stared at the three metal hooks at the end of Katz's right arm. The Phoenix Force commander had blocked the rifle stroke with his prosthesis. The hooks had snapped around the barrel like a bear trap.

Katz quickly jammed the muzzle of the Interarms silencer into the terrorist's hip and triggered the Uzi. A semijacketed wadcutter pierced flesh and muscle to burst bone. The WAFN flunky screamed and immediately fell to the floor in a quivering lump. Katz easily wrenched the M-14 from the wounded man's grasp and kicked him in the side of the head. The terrorist uttered a sigh, as if thankful to slip into unconsciousness.

KARL HAHN FELT as if the raid had suddenly passed him by. He had been forced to dive into the alley to avoid being blown to bits by enemy grenades. Then he had to duck behind the building when Manning blasted the side door with C-4.

James and McCarter seemed to have taken care of business upstairs and Manning and Katz were cleaning house on the first floor. That left only the side entrance, which led to the restaurant kitchen. Hahn aimed his MP-5 at the door and cautiously approached.

Two figures suddenly burst from the opening. Both men were armed and neither was a member of Phoenix Force. That was all Hahn had to know. He opened fire with the Heckler & Koch blaster. Parabellums stitched a bloody diagonal across the first terrorist's chest. The second man caught two bullets in the face. One 9 mm slug split his cheekbone, while the other burst his right eyeball and drilled through to his brain.

Hahn carefully peered into the kitchen. The bodies of three terrorists littered the tile floor, victims of the explosion that had blown the door off its hinges. The BND agent slowly crossed the threshold. The kitchen was not as large as he would have guessed. There were not many places to hide.

The kitchen was equipped with a standard professional dishwashing machine. Stacks of china plates and cups were sitting on the counter. A large table in the center of the kitchen was apparently where the meals were prepared. Ladles, colanders, knives, cleavers and meat mallets hung from a metal ring above the table.

A terrorist suddenly rose from beside the stoves. He held a Belgian-made Vigneron M-1 submachine gun with a 12-inch barrel. Hahn dropped to one knee by the cover of a table leg and triggered his MP-5. The terrorist's weapon barked. Bullets raked the tabletop. Splinters fell on Hahn's head and shoulders as he fired another burst at the enemy's position.

The shooting ceased. Hahn saw his opponent slide to the floor, his shirt drenched with blood. The BND agent rose slowly. He was surprised that his hands were steady when he removed the spent magazine from his H&K chopper. Hahn reached for a spare mag.

Herman Drache emerged from behind a large refrigerator, his Walther PPK held in a two-handed grip.

"Schweinhund," the United German National Party commander hissed as he aimed his pistol and squeezed the trigger.

The Walther clicked. The weapon had misfired.

Hahn quickly discarded his empty subgun and reached for the Walther P-5 autoloader in shoulder leather. Drache charged forward and launched a desperate roundhouse kick at the BND agent. Hahn's pistol cleared leather, only to be booted from his hand. Drache immediately slashed a karate chop at Hahn's throat. The side of his hand struck the agent on the side of the jaw.

The blow sent Hahn staggering backward into the sink. Drache grabbed a butcher knife from the utensils' rack and closed in for the kill. Hahn glanced about for a weapon. The only thing handy was the china. He rapidly seized two dinner plates and turned to face his opponent.

Drache almost felt sorry for Hahn. The BND agent stood his ground, waiting for the terrorist to attack. Drache moved the knife slowly, tracing small circles in the air with the point of the blade. Suddenly he raised the knife for a roundhouse slash.

The gesture was only a ploy. Drache's real attack was a karate snap-kick aimed for Hahn's groin. Taking out the BND agent would be easy when he was bent over in agony with his testicles ruptured. However, the plan did not work. Hahn blocked the kick by chopping the edge of a plate across Drache's shin. The UGNP leader grunted from the sharp pain that traveled up his leg. Drache immediately thrust the knife toward Hahn's stomach.

A plate slapped the blade, deflecting the knife. Hahn swung the other plate and smashed it against the side of Drache's face. China shattered on the terrorist's cheekbone. Drache's head spun from the blow and blood trickled from a minor cut below the left eye.

The terrorist tried to slash the butcher knife at his opponent, but Hahn quickly drew the broken plate under Drache's chin. He rammed the front of his elbow into the

UGNP ringleader's chest and shoved him backward. Drache adopted a knife fighter's stance and prepared to attack.

A flap of flesh opened at Drache's throat. Crimson blood vomited across his shirt. The terrorist stared at Hahn, amazed that the BND man had done so much harm with a dinner plate. Drache knew he was dying and he made no attempt to stop the blood that flowed from his severed carotid and jugular. He glanced at the scarlet stain on the broken edge of the dinner plate that Hahn still held in his fist. Drache uttered a sound that was meant to be a laugh. It became a death rattle.

The terrorist leader dropped his knife and fell against the table. His body slipped to the floor. Herman Drache twitched feebly and died.

As the Phoenix Force commandos started to regroup, McCarter, anger still seething within his body, said to Katz, "Well, that bloody well takes care of that, doesn't it?"

Katz surveyed the destruction, watching Calvin James and Karl Hahn doing one final recon of the dead. "Not quite," he said, turning to McCarter. "Not quite."

"You mean that bastard Weiss?" McCarter asked. "Let's get him now!"

The Israeli warrior shook his head slowly. As he slung his Uzi from his shoulder he started up the stairs to the second floor. "No, not today David. Weiss is a fish for another time."

23

Ten minutes after the firefight ended, the Lanterna Magika was surrounded by Czech soldiers and Prague police officers. No one knew what to do next. A number of civilian eyewitnesses claimed that they had heard a voice shout something in English through a megaphone. Then someone had threatened to use nuclear weapons. Yet all this had happened before the battle had reached its peak. Although it was once again quiet, no one was certain if it was safe or the battle within the restaurant was actually over.

Major Ladislav Svoboda stepped from his staff car and raised a megaphone to his lips. "I am with the Security Intelligence Service," he announced in English. "Please tell us what you want. I am certain we can come to an agreement."

"I certainly hope so," the amplified voice of Yakov Katzenelenbogen replied from the restaurant. "We've got some prisoners for you. They're terrorists who had threatened to use plutonium weapons. Maybe you heard about that."

"Yes," Svoboda replied awkwardly. "I'm confused. You say *you* are holding terrorists prisoner. Are they Americans?"

"Some are Americans and some are West German nationals, and all of them are fanatical lunatics," Katz explained. "However, none of them was carrying out the orders of any Western government."

"I see," Svoboda began. "Well, it sounds as if you've done quite a service for the Republic of Czechoslovakia. Why don't you come out so we can thank you?"

"Because we don't care to be arrested along with the terrorists," Katz replied. "You'd better warn those soldiers not to do anything rash. The plutonium is still here. My friends and I don't intend to launch the missiles, of course, but if a careless explosion or a rifle slug punctures the casing, we'll have a nasty radioactive leak."

"We don't want that," Svoboda agreed. "Would you object if I came in, so we could talk privately?"

"Certainly not," the Phoenix Force commander assured him through his megaphone. "But no tricks, please. We're trying to work through a rather awkward situation for all of us. Let's see if we can't solve everything without adding to the conflict."

"I agree," the major replied as he drew a 7.65 mm M-27 pistol from a holster under his jacket. He placed the weapon on the hood of his car. "I'm unarmed." Svoboda handed the megaphone to one of his men and walked toward the restaurant.

"We're not," Katz replied. "But don't worry."

"Sure," Svoboda muttered as he wiped the perspiration from his forehead.

The STB officer stepped through what remained of the front door. He gasped at the sight of shattered furniture and bloodied corpses that littered the floor. Six battered and sickly-looking terrorists sat at the foot of a flight of stairs. Their ankles were bound and their hands were behind their backs, no doubt bound as well.

"Hell, mate," a voice announced from a corner of the room.

The voice startled Svoboda. He had not noticed the figure who sat on one of the few chairs that had not been wrecked by the explosions. The man sat in the shadows, positioned so he could watch the door and the six captives. An Ingram machine pistol rested in his lap.

"Those blokes are the terrorists," David McCarter explained. "They don't feel too well right now. Probably feel chattier later."

"And who are you?" the major asked.

"Doesn't really matter what my name is," McCarter answered. "I'm not the diplomatic corps, either. Fellow you should talk to is upstairs."

"I'm coming down," Katz announced as he descended the stairs. "Just finished making a couple of phone calls."

"Phone calls?" Svoboda raised his eyebrows as the middle-aged, one-armed man with the Uzi subgun slung over his shoulder approached.

"Yes," Katz confirmed. "I've talked with the American ambassador, the ambassadors from Great Britain and the Federal Republic of Germany and the Soviet ambassador. I also managed to contact the president of Czechoslovakia and the first secretary. They're either coming here or sending representatives."

"Why?" Svoboda asked, more confused than ever.

"Because we want everyone to know that the terrorists are fanatics without any connection to Western governments, even though they carry American or German passports," Katz explained. "We're connected with such governments, and we don't want this turned into a propaganda tool."

"I'm rather glad the KGB isn't here," Svoboda commented.

"They will be," Katz said. "I told you I called the Soviet Embassy."

"I hope you called them last," the Czech said with a grin.

"Oh, yes," Katz said with a smile. "We'd appreciate some help with this. In fact, we don't mind if the truth is twisted a bit to officially read as a cooperative effort by East and West to save thousands of innocent people and prevent World War III."

"Sounds good," Svoboda said with a nod. "What about the plutonium?"

"A friend of mine checked the missiles with a Geiger counter," Katz answered. "The plutonium is safe for now, but you'd better get reliable people to haul it out of Prague."

"Speaking about getting out of Prague," the Czech major mused. "I suppose you fellows would like to slip out of the country without the KGB's knowledge?"

"We'd appreciate that," Katz confirmed.

"Do you think you can trust me?" Svoboda inquired.

"Trust isn't part of our profession," Katz said with an amused laugh. "After all, we are on opposite sides politically."

"But you and your friends have done quite a service for Czechoslovakia," Svoboda said with a shrug. "That's more than I can say for the KGB. I love my country. I wouldn't want to dishonor it by turning you over to the Soviets. That would be a disgraceful way to repay an act of friendship."

"If you could help us get out of Prague, we can get across the border on our own," Katz replied.

"When the ambassadors and the party officials arrive, you and your men should duck into the alley. I'll have a truck waiting for you. Head west on Nerudova. You have my word that you will not be stopped within the city limits."

"Things could go badly with you and your perfumed uncle," Katz warned.

"My KGB control?" Svoboda smiled. "He'll be busy trying to find some way to take some of the credit for crushing the recent wave of terrorism in Czechoslovakia. Remember, we all worked together on this. Right? I only wish we really had. This was one time we were all on the same side."

"I wish we could have handled this mission differently," Katz told him. "Maybe next time."

"Maybe," Svoboda said with a nod. "I'd better get that truck ready for you. Good luck."

COMING IN JUNE!

JACK ADRIAN

DEATH LANDS

**When all is lost,
there's always the future.**

The world blew out in 2001.

On a crisp clear January day, a presidential inauguration day, a one-megaton blast ripped through the Soviet embassy in Washington, D.C., power base of the United States and political center of the Western world.

Simultaneous explosions around the globe changed the face and shape of the earth forever. Out of the ruins emerges Deathlands, a world that conspires against survival.

In this hostile environment of strontium swamps and nuclear night, Ryan Cawdor, a survivalist and warrior, teams up with the beautiful Krysty Wroth and armorer J. B. Dix in an adventure to unlock the secrets of the pre-war scientific experiments that may hold the answer to survival in the Deathlands of the future.

DL-1

**A new thriller from a master
of psychological suspense!**

RAYMOND OBSTFELD

MASKED DOG

A decade ago, the Pentagon searched for a
volunteer to test a drug that would suppress
fear in human beings.

They found their guinea pig: Dr. Gifford S.
Devane, a convicted wife beater and child
abuser sentenced to twenty-five years in jail.

This imprisoned "volunteer" proved that
the drug worked only too well. Under the
Masked Dog Project, he became entirely
fearless, turning into a monster of
superhuman strength, a beast with an
uncontrollable sex drive. Only the jail's bars
protected society from an unprecedented
and terrifying menace.

Until Devane escaped.

Now the Masked Dog is loose. His targets:
the government people who created him, the
enemy agents who want him for his secret,
and—just for the thrill of it—anybody
whose innocence turns him on. . . .

**Watch for *Masked Dog* in August from
Gold Eagle Books, the #1 publisher
of adventures.**

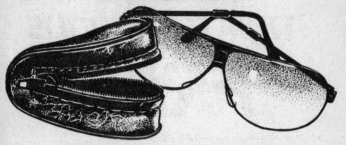

Take
4 explosive books
plus a
mystery bonus
FREE

Mail to **Gold Eagle Reader Service**

In the U.S.
P.O. Box 1396
Buffalo, N.Y. 14240-1396

In Canada
P.O. Box 2800, Station A
5170 Yonge St.,
Willowdale, Ont. M2N 6J3

YEAH! Rush me 4 free Gold Eagle novels and my free mystery bonus. Then send me 6 brand-new novels every other month as they come off the presses. Bill me at the low price of $2.25 each— a 10% saving off the retail price. There are no shipping, handling or other hidden costs. There is no minimum number of books I must buy. I can always return a shipment and cancel at any time. Even if I never buy another book from Gold Eagle, the 4 free novels and the mystery bonus are mine to keep forever.

Name _____ (PLEASE PRINT)

Address _____ Apt. No. _____

City _____ State/Prov. _____ Zip/Postal Code _____

Signature (If under 18, parent or guardian must sign)

This offer is limited to one order per household and not valid to present subscribers. Price is subject to change.

166-BPM-BP6S

4E-SUB-1-R